EVIL IN SUMMERLAND

Evil in Summerland

AN ABC FILES MYSTERY

Paul Masson

Paul Robert Masson

ISBN 978-1-7382730-1-0
Publisher Paul Robert Masson, PO Box 1866, Niagara-on-the-Lake, ON L0S 1J0, Canada

First Printing in this format, 2024

The ABC Files

by Paul Masson

eBooks

Hamish Cameron Investigates
A Chorus of Evil
Evil Through the Spyglass
Evil Ever Lives
Evil in Summerland
Memories of Evil

in Paperback

The ABC Files: A Collection of Three Novels
Evil Ever Lives
Evil in Summerland
Memories of Evil

Contents

Author's Notes

I am grateful to the Niagara-on-the-Lake Writers' Circle and my wife Betsy for helpful comments.

The organization that is central to the story, the African Post-Colonial Technical Institute, or APTI, is imaginary, as is the African Country of Summerland. The characters in this book are fictitious. Any resemblance to persons living or dead is accidental.

ASHCROFT-BY-THE-SEA, SEPT. 10

Stanfield the cat was bored. He hesitated about a nap on the window sill, then jumped onto Sean's lap instead. When the phone rang and Sean got up to answer it, he was dumped on the floor. Stanfield meowed in an annoyed tone and slunk away.

"Cameron and Carroll, Investigations," Sean said in a measured voice. "Sean Carroll speaking."

"Hello, this is Kevin Armbrister. My daughter Amelia has disappeared, and I don't have a clue where she's gone. You've got to try to find her!"

"I'll need some details. How old is she? Does she live at home?"

"She's 25, and has been studying at Eastern University. But when I tried calling her, her phone wasn't in service, and she's no longer on campus. Can you come to my office in Halifax tomorrow, so I can give you a photo and other information about her?"

"OK, I can do that."

Sean made a note of the address, and went back to his crossword puzzle. When his business partner, Hamish Cameron, came in, he explained that they had a new client. "Finally, some business. I'm going out of my mind with boredom."

Hamish, a retired judge, lived with Sean in The Oaks, where the detective agency was also located, in the picturesque Nova Scotia town of Ashcroft-by-the-Sea. "Another missing person case. I hope this doesn't turn out to be an abduction again!"

"Who knows? Anyway, I'll be driving to Halifax tomorrow to meet with this fellow, Armbrister. Apparently he's the CEO of a mining company, Truro Resources, with operations all over the world."

"Never heard of it."

"Well, it's big. Operations in Canada, Africa, and South America."

"You'll have to handle it. I'm going to be working on the fraud case. You could drop me off at the university. Izzie will be bringing me up to speed." Isabel French, Hamish's lady friend, was a professor of law at Dalhousie University, specializing in financial issues.

HALIFAX AND EASTERN UNIVERSITY, SEPT. 11

Sean drove to the Bond Building on Spring Garden Road for his appointment with Kevin Armbrister, and parked on the street. Hamish got out there too, since Izzie's office was a short walk away. "I'll get a ride back with her. She's got some things to do near Ashcroft."

Sean took the elevator up to a suite of offices leased by Truro Resources. The receptionist showed him through to Armbrister's office. Sean admired the nice view over the Citadel, the room's Persian carpets, and its antique mahogany furniture.

Armbrister got up and walked around his desk to shake Sean's hand. He was of medium height, seemingly in his late 40s or early 50s, and radiated energy. He sported a smile, which, though it seemed sincere, was clearly aimed at ingratiating himself with his guest.

"Glad you could come. Let me explain the situation. My daughter's studying for a Master's degree in International Relations at Eastern University. At least she was. When I looked her up recently she was no longer living on campus, and I don't know where she is now." He wrung his hands, obviously distressed.

"When did you last see her?"

"We had an argument a few months ago and we stopped talking to each other. I told her that her boyfriend was a loser, and she left in a huff. We were having dinner in a restaurant here in town. She hasn't phoned or texted me since. I had a change of heart, so I went over to EU to see if we could make things up. But I couldn't find her."

Armbrister gave Sean a photo, which showed an attractive young woman with reddish-brown hair and sparkling eyes.

"So where is home for her, where did she grow up?"

"As the name of the company suggests, I live in Truro. I moved to Canada from Britain when I was a lad, studied geology at university, worked for a mining company here in Canada, and then started my own business. The wife and I built a home near the Minas Basin, and that's where Amelia was raised. She's lived in Nova Scotia all her life, except for about a year when we moved to Africa and lived in Balabo, the capital of Summerland, where my company's first big mining operation was getting going."

"So you commute to the office from Truro every day?"

"I also have an apartment here in town, where typically I stay during the week, returning home on weekends."

"Could she have gone back to Truro? Or is there someone else she could be staying with, say a close friend or a relative?"

"If she was in Truro, I'd know about it. As for relatives, most of mine are in Britain. Amelia's mother and I are divorced–it's been a dozen years now–and she lives in BC. I checked with her and she says she hasn't seen or heard from Amelia for months."

Sean scratched his head. "Well, I guess I'd better start by poking around Eastern University, hoping to find someone who knows her who can tell me where she is. Let me have the address where she lived last. Don't you have a mobile number for her, and an email address?"

"I'll write out the last contact info I have for Amelia. Unfortunately the email address she used to have no longer works, and I don't know what happened to her phone."

"OK, that'll do for now. I'll keep you informed of what I learn as I proceed. You just want me to locate her, or do you want me to set up a meeting with you? Oh, and I'll need a retainer of a thousand dollars to start."

Armbrister wrote out a cheque to the detective agency. He added: "Just tell her that I'm sorry for our spat and I hope we can make it up soon." He seemed to be in pain, as if nursing an ulcer.

Sean sympathized. Though not a father, he was reminded of losing touch with a cousin because of some trivial disagreement. He said goodbye and drove the 50 kilometres to Eastern University, which was located in a new town southwest of Halifax that had grown up around the university following its construction on vacant land in the 1960s.

He used Google Maps to locate the address that Armbrister had given him for Amelia's former lodging. It was an apartment in a two story building a few blocks from the campus. The building looked to have been built within the last 20 years, but Sean noted signs of inadequate upkeep, such as unpainted window frames and sagging gutters. *Probably typical of housing rented out to students who aren't too picky about appearances or comfort*, Sean thought.

The outside door to the building was unlocked, and it gave access to a lobby with a set of buzzers with names and apartment numbers next to them. Sean didn't see any with the name "Armbrister." He buzzed one at random. Receiving no response, he tried another. A woman's voice came out over the intercom: "Hello. What is it?"

"I'm looking for Amelia Armbrister. Do you know where I can find her?"

"She doesn't live here anymore."

"Did she leave a forwarding address?"

"Ask Pamela in apartment 2A. She might know." The intercom gave a loud click as the connection was cut off.

Sean buzzed 2A but got no answer. He made a mental note to try her again later. In the meantime, he walked to the office of the International Relations Department. He'd picked up a campus map, which showed its location to be only a few hundred metres away. It was in a four-story plain stone building. According to the directory at the entrance, it also housed Political Science and Economics. International Relations was on the fourth floor.

The receptionist, a slender woman in her thirties with dark brown hair and glasses, was typing away at her desktop's keyboard when Sean entered the department chair's outer office.

A name plate on her desk identified her as Kelly Shields. She looked up, and asked him what she could do for him.

"I'm trying to find Amelia Armbrister, who was enrolled in a Master's program in International Relations." He gave her his card. "I was hired by her father, who's lost touch with her. Can you help?"

She frowned. "We're not allowed to give out information about any of our students."

"I realize that. But if I can't locate her for him then her father will have no choice but to make a missing person report. This wouldn't reflect well on the university, would it Kelly?" Sean gave her a fixed stare.

The receptionist looked flustered. "No, I guess not. Well, I can tell you this: she's still enrolled in the program, but taking time off her studies. I don't know where she's gone, but you might talk to her supervisor, Professor Fritz. He might be able to help you. He's in office 423."

Sean knocked on the door to 423 and entered after he heard "Come In!" Thomas Fritz was a small man, with thinning grey hair and sporting wire-rim glasses. He was obviously surprised to see that the visitor was not a graduate student or a colleague. He peered up from his desk at Sean.

Sean gave a smile intended to disarm the professor. "I'm trying to find Amelia Armbrister on behalf of her father. I gather she's suspended her studies for the moment. Can you tell me why, and whether she's still living on campus?"

The other man paused for a moment, then asked: "What's your interest in all this? And what does Amelia's father want to do once he knows where she is? Anyway, I can tell you in general terms that she was working on a thesis for me, but decided it was going nowhere so she wanted some time off to think about another topic."

"Mr. Armbrister hired me to try to find where she is, so he can contact her. That's all."

Fritz sighed. "I'm afraid I can't give you her exact address. She's in Africa, in Summerland, revisiting the country where she lived for a year when she was a kid."

"What is she doing there?"

Fritz stood up, as if lecturing a class. "She's studying the actions of the Western powers and what used to be called the Communist Bloc in trying to align African countries on their side, whether through carrots or sticks. Summerland is a particular case of the failure of the Western model of free enterprise and openness to trade and capital markets. Although the country, located on the Indian Ocean near the equator, prospered from its trade links with Europe and North America, it turned its back to the West after an Islamic coup installed a military government, and it is now gravitating towards the Chinese orbit."

Sean stopped him. "All right, all right, but why does she think it's necessary to go there?"

"Amelia felt that merely repeating the known facts about Summerland wasn't sufficient for her thesis. She hopes to dig up some new material that would help us to understand why the country turned against the West."

"Isn't that dangerous? She could be considered a spy!"

"That's what I told her, but she was determined to go. Under the circumstances, I've asked that she find a new supervisor if and when she returns. I don't want to be responsible for her. If she gets in trouble, maybe even ends up in prison, there's nothing I can do for her, but I'll get blamed if I sanctioned her trip." He looked away, realizing how cowardly this must seem. "I hoped that this would dissuade her from going, but it didn't."

"So you're not in touch at all? Do you have any idea where she was planning to stay, or who she hoped to talk to?"

"Not really. She lived in the capital when she was young, and I expect that's where she would have started. Apparently there's only one decent hotel in Balabo now. Why don't you contact them to find out if she's staying there?"

"Do you hear from her occasionally? Is there anyone else who's still in touch with her, who might have her present location?"

Fritz shook his head. "I really wouldn't know. I gather she's given up her lodging. I haven't heard from her since she left for Summerland a few weeks ago."

Sean walked back to her apartment building. It was now lunch time, so he thought he might have a better chance of finding Pamela in. He rang her buzzer again, and was rewarded with a squawk from the intercom. "Hello?"

"I'm looking for Amelia Armbrister, and I gather that she's in Summerland now. Do you have a way of contacting her?"

"So who are you?"

"I'm searching for her on behalf of her father, who's lost touch with her."

"OK, I'll be right down."

Pamela was a woman in her mid-twenties with brown hair tied back in a bun. Despite lack of makeup and jeans and a flannel shirt, Sean found her very attractive. She explained that she was a PhD student in International Relations as well as a former neighbour of Amelia's. "I'm probably her best friend here. She asked me to pick up her mail for her."

"Do you stay in touch with her? Does she have a mobile phone or an email address?"

"Yes, she texted me to say that she bought a phone after arriving in Summerland. That's the only way I have to reach her. Wi-Fi isn't available, and she doesn't have an internet connection or email." She showed Sean her phone with the contact for Amelia, and Sean wrote it down.

"Is she there alone? Isn't she worried about her safety?"

Pamela looked uneasy, and didn't reply directly to his questions. "She thought she'd be fine, and hasn't told me of any problems since she got there. It's a pretty strict society, so she's not in much danger. Of course she has to wear long dresses and a face covering. I don't think that she's allowed to drive, but that doesn't matter much, she can take a taxi or a bus."

She took out a magnetic card from her pocket to get back into her apartment.

Sean decided not to bother her further. He gave her his business card. "Please let me know if you hear from her again. Oh, can I also get your phone number? Just in case I fail to connect with Amelia."

Pamela paused, and reluctantly agreed. "I'll just call the cell number on your card, so you'll have it on your phone."

He thanked her and walked back to his car and drove home.

ASHCROFT AND HALIFAX, SEPT. 12

Back in Ashcroft Sean filled Hamish in about his visit to Eastern University.

Hamish was intrigued. "You know I spent some time in Summerland in the 1990s! I was seconded to the African Postcolonial Technical Institute, the brainchild of Lester Pearson, which is located in Ottawa. The APTI was established to give technical assistance on governance issues to African countries upon their obtaining political independence. I served two years as assistant legal counsel, working on such issues as the drafting of national constitutions and setting up judicial systems. Summerland was one of the countries I worked on, helping to train magistrates, and I went there frequently. So, as it happens, I know Balabo pretty well–though it undoubtedly has changed since then."

"I had no idea! How did that happen?"

"Well, I'd become a judge here in Nova Scotia, and one of the lawyers at my old firm who was now working at APTI gave me a call to see if I was interested in filling a vacancy there, because they needed someone to give advice to African countries on legal matters. Bob Wismer was his name. He talked me into taking a leave of absence, so I moved to Ottawa for two years, though I spent much of my time in Africa. It was a great learning experience. I have good memories of that time. I really thought my work made a difference."

"Interesting ... Anyway, I'm meeting with Armbrister again in Halifax. I'll tell him what I discovered at Eastern University and ask him where we go from here. In the meantime, I tried texting and calling Amelia in Summerland, but her phone doesn't seem to be connected to the network. It's hard to be sure, because I understand that the sole mobile provider in the country is often out of commission."

*****

Armbrister was looking at a computer screen when Sean entered his office. He jumped up and motioned for Sean to sit on the couch next to his desk, and joined him there.

"So, have you been able to contact Amelia? Where is she now?"

"She's working on getting a topic for her Master's thesis. She's doing field work in Summerland, but I haven't been able to talk to her. Either her phone is off or the network is down."

"Summerland, eh? I remember it well. If it weren't for the fact that I had to leave the country as persona non grata I'd go back there and look for her myself. The mining operation I developed in west Summerland has been closed, but I hear the Chinese may be interested in the lithium carbonate deposits. I'd like to find out something about that. Can you go to Summerland yourself?"

"Let me consult with Hamish Cameron, my partner, and get back to you. You realize that travel expenses alone will run into the tens of thousands of dollars?"

Armbrister shrugged. "Money's no object. After all, I only have one daughter!"

Sean promised to get back to Armbrister within 24 hours and returned to Ashcroft.

*****

Hamish was dubious that it made sense for Sean to go to Balabo just to find Amelia. "Let me call my friend Bob Wismer, he may know what the situation is like there. He might even know someone who could recommend a local private detective to look for her. We'll see what he says."

Bob was now working at Canada's Department of Justice. Hamish hadn't talked to him directly for years, but they exchanged Christmas cards. He called Bob's number.

"Hamish, you old dog, how are you? I gather you reached mandatory retirement age as a judge and became a private detective–that's an interesting career progression! So, what are you up to?"

"Strangely enough, my stint at APTI may come in handy in my current case, because we are trying to find a mining executive's daughter who is somewhere in Summerland – at least we think she is. Do you keep in touch with your former colleagues at APTI? And do you know anyone with contacts in Balabo? If we're lucky, we might find someone on the spot who could try to locate the daughter, and at least reassure the father that she's OK."

"Tell you what, if you leave it with me I'll check around, though as you know APTI no longer keeps up relations with Summerland's government. It's good you called when you did, though, because as it happens I'm hosting a retirement party for Francis Chastain next week. Why don't you join us at my cottage?"

Chastain, an Englishman, was for a long time the noted head of APTI's legal department, under whom Hamish had worked years before. He'd occupied a largely honorary post for the past dozen years, and now was finally retiring from the Institute.

"Sure, that would be great! It'll give me a chance to catch up with the old guard, and maybe learn something useful about Summerland. You know, I had a great deal of respect for Francis and I enjoyed working for him. He was knowledgeable and dedicated to helping African countries as best he could."

Bob explained that it would be a small party, only half a dozen guests were invited, all people Hamish probably remembered from when he'd worked there in the mid-1990s. Bob's expansive cottage, which Hamish remembered from his time in Ottawa, had magnificent views of the Gatineau River and was located on a large treed lot that descended from the road down to the water's edge.

"Feel free to stay a day or two with me. No point in looking for a hotel, there aren't any nearby. I'll pick you up at the airport. Just send me your itinerary when you have it."

*****

Sean called Kevin Armbrister to explain that they were exploring alternative ways of locating Amelia that did not involve a trip to Balabo.

Armbrister was impatient. "I can't wait forever! If you don't make any progress by next week, then either you or Hamish gets on the plane or I will do so myself–damn the torpedoes!"

OTTAWA AND GATINEAU, SEPT. 16

It was a pleasant mid-September day when Hamish took the non-stop WestJet flight from Halifax to Ottawa. After about two hours in the air, he disembarked at MacDonald-Cartier airport and walked to the exit, skipping the luggage carousels since he'd just packed a carryon bag for his short stay in Ottawa.

Bob was waiting inside the doors that led to the parking lot, holding a sign just in case they had trouble recognizing each other after so many years. In the event, he picked Hamish out from the crowd, a tall, stately man with grey hair and an air of authority. Bob waved, and Hamish strode over with a smile on his face.

They walked out to Bob's red Mustang and headed north, taking the Parkway to Bronson and over the Portage Bridge into Quebec. After leaving the town of Gatineau behind they turned onto a winding two-lane road through woods and up and down hills to Bob's cottage, located on the west side of the Gatineau River.

"I remember this," Hamish said. "It's really very beautiful here, and so secluded! You wouldn't know that you're half an hour from the nation's capital."

Bob turned down his long driveway, which led to a rustic A-frame perched on a knoll over the river. A path with steps cut in the rock went down to the water. Hamish could see that several of the guests were enjoying a swim, and he rushed to change into his swimsuit. He started down the steep path to the water, waving to the others who were already there. He thought he recognized two of them, but he skipped the introductions and jumped into the river from the float which was tied up to Bob's dock.

Bob shouted to them to enjoy, then went back to the house to finish his preparations for the party. Francis Chastain, who lived in Ottawa, would be driving up around seven and not staying the night. The other guests would have plenty of time to shower and dress for dinner before his arrival.

With Labour Day in the rear view mirror, the days were getting noticeably shorter so that at five o'clock the sun was already behind the trees on the bank and the air was starting to feel fresh. The swimmers reluctantly climbed onto the float and shook the water off themselves like Labrador retrievers, grabbed towels, and headed back up the hill. Hamish caught up to one of them, a man whose naked torso showed that he kept fit, despite his age, and stuck out his hand. "Hi, I'm Hamish Cameron, I don't know if you remember me. You're Roger Boudreau, aren't you? We were at APTI at the same time, in the mid-1990s. Did you stay there long after that?"

"Oh, Hamish, of course!" he answered in his gracious manner, with a slight French accent. "No, like you I suppose, I was seconded for a fixed term, in my case three years. Afterward, I went back to Paris to my job at the French development agency, the AFD. I retired two years ago."

"So, what brings you to Canada? Did you make a special trip for Chastain's retirement party?" Hamish softened the directness of his question with an apologetic laugh.

"Actually, I have a contract with Global Affairs Canada. I keep wanting to call it CIDA, but that got folded into a larger ministry a long time ago. They aren't very well represented in francophone Africa, so I oversee a couple of projects for them. Even in retirement, I feel I have a duty to continue to help out."

Arriving at the cottage, Hamish and Roger repaired to their respective bedrooms to change. The upstairs had three bedrooms, two facing the front, and the master bedroom at the back, facing the river. Hamish pushed open the door to his and was surprised to find it already occupied by a small man with a thin frame who was donning a shirt. "Oops, sorry, I should have knocked. I guess we are sharing the room–I did notice that there were two beds, but I wasn't sure that they would both be occupied. Let me introduce myself: I'm Hamish Cameron."

The other man stuck out his hand: "Clarence Chen. I used to work at APTI, and Bob was kind enough to invite me to this party for Francis Chastain, a man whom I admire and who was my boss. I've kept in touch with him over the years and I never miss the opportunity when I'm in Canada to look him up."

"So where are you based?"

"I'm a professor of Political Science at the National University of Singapore, but I'm visiting Carleton University here for the fall term."

Clarence finished dressing and left the room to Hamish, who quickly showered and dressed in a light blue dress shirt, which he left unbuttoned at the top, and grey slacks. He then went down the stairs to the joint living/dining open area with its large fireplace, to meet his other colleagues.

In their work at APTI, Hamish and his co-workers spent a lot of time in the field, often going on missions together. Thus they got to know each other in different, less formal contexts, forming close friendships or, in some cases, strong antipathies. The reunion reminded Hamish of the camaraderie that he had experienced at the time.

Hamish recalled that Bob had said that he had invited six people to the party: Francis Chastain and Hamish, plus four others, all of whom had worked at APTI in the mid-1990s. They consisted of three men–Roger Boudreau, Clarence Chen, and John Kamara–plus a Canadian woman, Jessica Bowles. Kamara was a Liberian jurist. Bowles, like Bob Wismer, at present worked for the Canadian government.

Jessica arrived a little before seven, parking her car close to the cottage. Since she lived in Ottawa like Francis Chastain she was not spending the night but would drive home after the party.

Bob walked outside and greeted her warmly, kissing her on both cheeks. "Jessica, great to see you! I expect that you remember everyone, but just in case, I'll introduce our other guests to you."

Hamish remembered Jessica as someone he had not worked closely with but who had been a friend when he worked at APTI. Jessica recognized him right away and gave him a hug. "It's great to see you again, Hamish."

"Likewise, Jessica." Hamish thought she had aged well. Her face was unlined and her hair was attractively styled. She wore a discreet scent that he found alluring.

The group was now complete except for the guest of honour. Bob took drink orders and went to the bar to pour out cocktails, beer and wine. In the meantime, the other guests made conversation about their recent activities and recollections of their past interactions, when they were twenty years younger and were excited to be working on issues where they thought they could make a difference. Many of their reminiscences concerned the countries where they worked. Roger Boudreau talked about his attempts to steer the economic policies of the West African francophone countries onto a sustainable path. Jessica Bowles recalled the struggle against apartheid. The APTI had worked behind the scenes to broker the power-sharing agreement between Nelson Mandela and FW de Klerk which eventually led to the election of Mandela as president of the Republic of South Africa in 1994. Clarence Chen spoke of the advice on land redistribution he had given to the government of Zimbabwe, which unfortunately had been ignored by its president, Robert Mugabe.

Hamish brought up the work he had done with Francis Chastain in Rwanda after the genocide and the victory of the Tutsi forces led by Paul Kagame, which overthrew the Hutu government. Hamish helped to draft a new constitution and set of laws that removed any official reference to a person's ethnicity and outlawed organizations identifying with one or the other ethnic group. "I felt that we were making a real difference, helping the country recover from a horrific experience of internecine violence. I learned a lot from Francis, who guided me in my work. He clearly has an unparalleled grasp of the complexities of constitutional law as it relates to individual rights."

John Kamara, a former colleague who was now a senior government official in his native Liberia, bemoaned the fact that despite some progress, many African countries still suffered from poor governance and undemocratic regimes. "Colonialism has cast a long shadow. But could the APTI have done better? Did we help to prop up dictators by giving them the patina of legitimacy?"

At this point Francis Chastain arrived. He was looking a bit frail as he got out of his car and walked with a slight limp to the cottage's front door, a tall, thin figure dressed in a grey suit. Bob had kept an eye out for him so was waiting there and greeted him warmly. "Welcome to our little get-together in your honour." He took Chastain around the room, mentioning the name of each guest in turn and details of their involvement with APTI.

Before inviting his guests to proceed to dinner, Bob insisted on making a toast to the guest of honour, and brought out two bottles of Veuve Clicquot and champagne flutes. He filled the flutes one by one and passed them out. "To our distinguished guest, with our best wishes for your well-merited retirement!"

The other guests rose and drank to his health, their faces showing the veneration that he had inspired in his staff over his long career. Jessica Bowles took a picture of the assembled group, promising to send each of them a print.

After a few other toasts and some polite chit chat, Bob invited everyone to move to the buffet table, where were laid out cold hors d'oeuvres, consisting of several dips and smoked salmon canapes, warm entrees that included paella, mac and cheese, and a beef stew, and a selection of salads, followed by pastries and fruit served in bowls.

The guests balanced their plates on their knees or found tables on which to rest them. Conversation lagged for a while as they ate, then they returned to the discussion they were having when Chastain arrived.

John came back to the charge: "Did APTI fail in its task of improving governance in post-colonial Africa? After more than 60 years of independence, the continent is still run by dictators and plagued by wars and famines. Couldn't we have done better?"

There was an awkward silence. The others turned to Francis Chastain to get his authoritative view on this question, since he was the most senior member of the group and had continued to work at the organization after the others had left.

Chastain paused to consider, then answered: "One can always do better, but the difficulty is to formulate a coherent policy that is even-handed, respects national sovereignty and can rally support both within the country concerned and among the donor countries. Even in retrospect, that's a daunting task. "

Kamara was not to be deflected by such an easy excuse, however valid. He shook his head. "I think we can look to a success story, South Africa, where pressure from Western governments and sanctions against the apartheid government eventually led to a change in regime, and ask why the US and Europe did not use a similar strategy with despots in the Democratic Republic of Congo, Angola, or Chad? To my mind, the answer is obvious: they viewed those countries' strategic position and wealth of natural resources as being more important than the welfare of their inhabitants!"

Roger Boudreau disagreed: "South Africa was unique because it was a surviving example of white rule over a predominantly black population. The other African countries you mention are regimes run by blacks, and Western countries are wary of being seen to interfere with them."

Clarence Chen, the Singaporean political scientist, inter-jected: "In any case, we were talking about APTI's role. We're not to blame for the mistakes of governments, either Western or African!"

Hamish disagreed: "I wonder if it's that clear cut. After all, the APTI is an agency run by Western governments. It is they who call the shots, whether or not representatives of African countries serve on the board, because the former pay the bills."

Bob asked: "So, what happened in Summerland? Was it our fault? I'll remind you of the basic facts. A former Italian colony, it became a joint protectorate of France and Britain after WWII, and achieved full independence in 1958. It was one of the first countries to benefit from APTI's technical assistance. APTI helped write its constitution and set up a competition bureau, designed a value-added tax to replace high tariffs, and advised the Summerlanders to establish a duty-free zone which became a magnet for companies making clothing from Egyp-tian and Indian cotton and exporting it around the world. The government offered favourable terms to multinationals willing to move their head offices to Summerland. As a result of all of this, the country, though starting at the same level as its neighbours, soon was much more prosperous. Summerland became the poster child for liberal economic policies and the success story that the APTI would cite when describing its activities.

"But in the late-1990s, the country moved from poster child to fallen angel. The army, which was well equipped thanks to the country's newfound wealth and the eagerness of Western countries to furnish it with modern weapons, ousted the democratically-elected government and set up a junta to run the country. It chased away many of the foreign companies and cut off most ties with the outside world. It instituted Sharia to replace an ineffective judicial system, making it popular with the mostly Islamic population. So all our work at APTI went down the drain. Where did we go wrong?"

With a sigh, Francis answered the question, which implicitly had been posed to him. "Ah, Summerland, the thorn in our side. Undoubtedly, we made mistakes. We overestimated the importance of laws, and underestimated the need to create effective institutions to enforce them. Sadly, the lesson we drew from this was to be even more demanding of the African governments we were advising, so that in the end they turned away from us and sought assistance elsewhere, particularly from China. The Chinese got things done and weren't too concerned about the niceties of laws, individual rights, and democratic accountability. Besides, they were willing to build the infrastructure that many African countries lacked. After Summerland, our stock in Africa fell. We were no longer welcome in many of the other countries of the continent. We've been struggling to justify our existence ever since, and I wouldn't be surprised if the US and the EU finally decided to pull the plug. If they withdrew their financial support, it would effectively shut us down."

Hamish hesitated to disagree with his mentor, but said tentatively: "I think the APTI served a useful purpose in the early years of independence in many countries. Now they're better able to adapt their institutions to their own customs and preferences. The APTI may no longer be needed. This seems to me to be a sign of its success, not failure." When he looked around the room, he could see that a few were nodding their heads, but most seemed unconvinced.

Bob cleared his throat and said, "I had another reason to invite you all here tonight. You probably don't know this, but I've been asked by the president of APTI to write a history of the institution. The president has given me complete access to the confidential files, which lay out details of our advice and technical assistance over the years. They're confidential primarily so as not to embarrass the governments concerned, but of course with the passage of time the raison d'être of confidentiality diminishes, and he told me I could draw on the files freely for my book." He took a sip of his drink, then continued: "But there's one thing I found in the files that concerns me, and I hope you can tell me what it means, since it refers to events in the mid-1990s. Interestingly, it involves Summerland.

"You may recall that we were asked by the Summerland government in 1993 to advise them on the steps needed to set up a casino in the capital, Balabo. The finance minister had been impressed by the success of Macau in using gaming as a source of government revenue. Its casinos provide well-paid employment, and the region boasts the highest per capita incomes in the world. The minister asked, couldn't the same thing be done in Summerland? The board of APTI discussed the issue before responding. Many of the European countries were sceptical. The US and Britain were more favourable to the idea, but they emphasized the need to beef up police surveillance in order to thwart any attempt of organized crime to get a foothold in the casino. The official report, transmitted on a confidential basis to the government, was inconclusive, but it did say that the APTI would not provide any technical assistance to facilitate its creation. As you no doubt remember, Summerland decided to go ahead with the project nevertheless. The decline of law and order in the country is now widely thought to have worsened markedly at that time, as the casino became a mecca for money laundering and prostitution. The outrage of the Muslim clerics eventually brought down the regime."

Hamish couldn't resist interjecting: "We know all that. But surely that was not APTI's fault, except to the extent that we could have been more definite in our warnings?"

Bob shook his head. "That brings me to the note I found in the files. Though we declined officially to get involved, it appears that we were helping to set up the casino behind the scenes. I found a note laying out the substantial budget of a project titled 'Ocean Pearl.' As you may recall, that was the name given to the casino that was built in Balabo. The note was labelled 'Confidential-Level 1'."

Hamish saw incredulity on Jessica's face, and he had the same reaction. "I had no idea! But then I started in 1994 and didn't work on matters related to the casino in Summerland. Isn't there someone still around who was in charge of our relations with the country at the time?"

"Unfortunately, no. The desk officer, Terence Deaver, retired in 1997 and passed away last year. I'm hoping one of you might have heard rumours, and can give me a lead to follow. I could just ignore the whole thing in my history of APTI, but that would be dishonest, and leaving it out would limit interest in the book."

Francis put his glass down and looked around the room before giving his opinion: "We don't know what the work consisted of, do we? Maybe it was designed to beef up law enforcement, after the government had decided to go ahead with the project against our wishes? Was there any mention of who was involved, or their area of expertise?"

Bob replied: "Unfortunately not. I can find no other reference in the files to this project."

"Well then, I don't see that it's worth mentioning in the APTI history. You don't even know that the name Ocean Pearl in the budget document refers to the casino. It could be a generic term for Summerland itself. I remember hearing it used that way occasionally, before the takeover by the military junta."

The others agreed with Chastain, and questioned the need to pursue the issue. Roger denied any knowledge of what had happened in Summerland: "I was spending most of my time working in Abidjan. I didn't even have time to read the newspapers—not that the local ones carried any news about Summerland anyway." John said that in the early 1990s he was working with the Nigerians to try to inch them toward democracy, and didn't follow events in East Africa. Jessica added her vote to ignoring the note in the file: "I was serving as an intermediary between Mandela and de Klerk. Summerland could have been a million miles away as far as I was concerned. Anyway, what's done is done, there's no point in making a big deal of our failure in Summerland."

The evening was capped by a series of toasts to Francis Chastain. Jessica left first, then Francis. Bob accompanied him out to his car, and Hamish heard them talking quietly for a few minutes, but couldn't make out what was said. After enjoying a last drink and chatting with the others about what they would do the next day, Hamish turned in.

GATINEAU, SEPTEMBER 17

Hamish soon was deep in the arms of Morpheus, but after two hours or so he got up to use the washroom–trying to be as quiet as possible to avoid waking Clarence–and was unable to get back to sleep. The pleasant weather of the day before had given way to strong winds that shook the trees surrounding the cottage, and then to a brief shower that pounded on the roof of the A-frame. After the cold front passed through, he was finally able to get back to a fitful sleep. He woke up again at around 5 am and noticed that the bed beside him was empty.

He tossed and turned for a while before rising and going downstairs to brew himself a coffee. He found Clarence at the kitchen table, reading from a set of loose leaf pages. "I couldn't sleep, so I got up early. With the twelve hour time difference with Singapore my body rhythms are completely screwed up! I'm working on my speech for a conference that I'm attending in Toronto."

"I won't distract you then." Hamish noticed that there was already a pot with fresh coffee in it, so he poured himself a cup and rooted around to find something to nibble on. In a bread basket there were a few breakfast rolls so he helped himself to one.

With nothing else to do, he decided to wander around the grounds as the sun was just rising over the trees on the east bank of the river. The ground was damp so he was careful where he walked. There was an open area of flat ground behind the cottage with a patio on which stood a round table and four chairs. Hamish paused there to look around. He could see down to the float from which he had jumped the day before. There seemed to be something bobbing in the water, but he couldn't make out what it was. He decided to have a look. Hamish carefully descended the steps so as not to slip.

When he reached the bottom, he recoiled. The corpse of a man clothed in pyjamas was floating face down. Hamish put his hand to his mouth to avoid vomiting. After his stomach settled, he thought he should attempt to pull the body up onto the dock. But it was clear from the smell that the man was dead, and Hamish did not want to contaminate what might be a crime scene. He reached for his phone and called 911. "There's a drowned man in the Gatineau River close to shore. Send the police!"

Hamish hurried back to the house, intending to wake Bob to inform him. Clarence was still working on his notes in the kitchen, but none of the others was up. Out of breath, Hamish croaked, "There's a body floating in the river! I've called the police. I'm going to wake Bob up to let him know." Chen looked up with alarm, but didn't say anything.

There were three bedrooms on the second floor. Roger and John shared one of them. Hamish knocked on the remaining one, but got no answer. He pushed open the door, and saw that the bed had been slept in but was empty. Hamish came to the awful realisation that the body was probably Bob's.

Hamish rushed down the stairs and reached the ground floor just as a police car and an EMT ambulance drew into the parking area in front of the cottage. A man in civilian clothes sporting a beer belly got out from the passenger seat of the police car with some difficulty and came over to Hamish: "Je suis l'Inspecteur André Giroux. C'est vous qui avez appelé?"

"That's right, I found the body and phoned 911." He pointed down to the float. "I'm afraid that it might be of the owner of the cottage, Robert Wismer."

The police and the paramedic proceeded down the stairs and examined the corpse, before carefully raising it and placing it in a body bag and then onto a stretcher. Able now to see his face, Hamish confirmed that it was indeed Bob's body.

Giroux made a cursory examination, which revealed a wound on his forehead, probably caused by either falling on or being hit by a rock. The police cordoned off the area around the dock while the corpse was awkwardly carried up the hill to the ambulance, which drove off. Then the inspector walked up to the cottage, where the guests were standing around the table on the patio.

"Est-ce que vous parlez français?" Giroux asked of the group. John shook his head. "OK, I'll switch to English. Can I have your names please?" He took out a notebook and looked expectantly, fixing his gaze first on Roger.

"Je suis Roger Boudreau. Je suis, ou plutôt j'étais, l'invité de Robert Wismer, à qui cette propriété appartenait."

"Vous êtes français?"

"En effet."

Giroux methodically took down the names of all of them and their relationships with the deceased. After he had done so, he asked: "Why did this guy--what's his name, Vismère?--leave the house during the night? Anyone hear something?"

They all shook their heads. Hamish explained that Bob had hosted a party for Francis Chastain, an Englishman who served in a senior position at an international agency located in Ottawa.

"Uh-oh. I'm going to have to coordinate with the RCMP about this. And I'm going to need to get some backup to check out the grounds. Maybe this was not an accident. In any case, you need to stay here so that we can interrogate you further."

Clarence Chen protested. "But I'm due in Toronto later today!"

"Sorry, but you're going to have to stay here for now. And don't leave the house. Someone will be coming to search the grounds for clues. I'll call them tout-de-suite."

The four of them returned to the kitchen and checked out what food was available for lunch. Fortunately, Bob had stocked the fridge with cold cuts, salads, and things to drink, and a bread drawer gave them a selection of rolls and chips. Each of them made his own sandwich and helped himself to a drink.

Hamish took a sip from one of the bottles of a craft beer left in the fridge. Addressing no one in particular, he said: "That was quite a storm last night! I didn't look at my watch, but I think it was about 2 am. I wonder if Bob got up to check outside that everything was OK."

John announced that he had slept like a lamb, and had not awakened until 7 am. Roger confirmed that, chuckling that his sleep had been disturbed by the storm but that John had kept snoring throughout. "After it passed I managed to sleep well, though. It seemed to reduce the humidity and to cool the air."

Hamish continued: "Bob would have left some footprints on the ground if he went out after the storm. The autopsy should give the police a good idea of when he died, and they will know when the storm came through. If he did go out after it rained, he might well have slipped on those steps and hit his head. He could have rolled into the water if he was unconscious. I noticed yesterday that there is an eddy near the dock, so he wouldn't have been swept down the river."

Clarence said hesitantly, "You know, now that I think of it, I did hear something, but I don't know if it was before the storm or afterward. I knew I wouldn't get to sleep otherwise, given my jet lag, so I took a couple of sleeping pills that knocked me out. But I awoke after they wore off, so I took another one. Then I heard the noise of an engine. I didn't think anything of it at the time, but it must have stopped here. I wonder if Bob went out to talk to whoever was in it. I was still groggy from the pills, and I must have drifted off again. I didn't hear the storm."

"Why would anyone come by at that time of night?" Hamish wondered. "We're a long way from anywhere, and I wouldn't want to navigate that winding road in the dark if I didn't have to."

Roger frowned. "Well, Francis and Jessica drove it to go back to their homes. I wonder if maybe one of them got into trouble and turned around, or left something important which they needed to retrieve from Bob's cottage."

"But they'd been gone for more than an hour. The party must have ended around midnight." Hamish shrugged. "It's a mystery that maybe the police will unravel. But if they determine that he died by falling, it won't really matter. By the way, I guess we should call Jessica and Francis to tell them what happened. And does anyone know if Bob had any close relatives we should contact?"

"Perhaps Jessica would know," Roger offered. "I think they may have been close friends at some point. I do know that Bob has been divorced for a number of years, and he has a son who lives abroad."

They found Jessica's number in Bob's Rolodex and Hamish gave her a call. "Jessica, hi, this is Hamish Cameron. It was good to see you last night at the party. I have terrible news, though. Bob has been found drowned in the river. The police are coming back to search the grounds, in case it was the result of foul play."

"Oh, no! That's awful! How did it happen? What can I do to help? Shall I call his former wife? He has a cousin as well who lives up the Ottawa Valley, and I could call him."

"That sounds like a good idea. Bob seems to have slipped on the wet ground and fallen into the water, but the police are still investigating. Did you get home OK last night, or did you get caught in the storm? It rained cats and dogs here."

"No, I got back home by one, and I must have been fast asleep when it came through. I didn't hear a thing."

Francis Chastain was shocked by the news. "To think one of his last acts was to host a party for me! Will the police want to interview me, do you know? In any case, I'll be reachable at this number."

*****

Inspecteur Giroux returned with two other police officers to search the grounds. This time they left their cruiser just off the road, and scoured the driveway and the small unpaved parking area next to the house for tire tracks. Aside from theirs, made earlier in the day, there were none that had not been mostly washed away by the storm in the early hours of the morning. The pair of Gatineau policemen spread out and walked through the brush around the house, coming up with a few discarded soda cans and cigarette butts, but nothing that looked recent. From there they proceeded down to the water, exploring the hill beside the path. There were several sets of footprints leading from the house to the steps down to the river, clearly made after the storm had passed. In addition to Hamish's, there were prints made earlier by Giroux and the paramedic, but no others.

At the water's edge, Giroux discovered a rock that looked as though it might have a trace of blood on it. It was resting in a pile of other stones, so it was impossible to tell whether it had been disturbed. He told his deputy to put it in a plastic evidence bag. "Let's see if they can match it with the dead man's DNA."

Returning to the house, Giroux entered the living room where the four guests were gathered. "Unless the autopsy suggests otherwise, it seems pretty clear that this guy Vismère died of natural causes. So you're free to go, but give me an address and a phone number where you can be reached. And keep me updated should you change locations."

Clarence Chen was the first to volunteer the information. "I'll be at the Westin in Toronto. If I hurry, I think I can make the last Porter flight and won't miss the opening dinner of my conference." He gave Giroux his cell phone number, before using his phone to call a cab.

The others followed suit. Roger Boudreau said that he still had business in Ottawa and would check into a hotel there. John Kamara decided to do the same and volunteered to share a cab with Roger. Hamish's flight back to Halifax wasn't until the next day. "I'll spend the night here, if that's OK. Then I'll be in Ashcroft-by-the-Sea, Nova Scotia. Here are phone numbers where I can be reached." He gave the inspector his business card.

"A detective, eh? Well, if we run out of clues we'll have to call you!" He laughed scornfully. "I guess you'll be all alone in the house. Is there someone who can lock it up when you leave? And who will be responsible for the dead man's estate?"

"According to Jessica Bowles, who was also at the party, a lawyer who was a close friend of Wismer's will be the executor. He will secure the cottage and his other property. He's been notified." Hamish gave Giroux the details.

*****

Hamish went around the house checking that windows were closed and lights were turned off, wanting to tidy up things before leaving the next day. Wismer's executor had agreed to give Hamish a lift to the airport and to lock up the place when he left.

The second floor had a small office in addition to the three bedrooms and a washroom. Hamish noticed an accordion file on top of the desk with the label "Summerland." Curious, he leafed through it. On top was the budgetary allocation for Ocean Pearl that Wismer had mentioned, dated May 13, 1995. The rest of the file was mostly official reports, including one addressed to the government indicating that APTI would not provide any technical assistance relative to the creation of a casino. It was dated March 15, 1994. The first page of the report listed the names of contributors. Hamish noted that Roger Boudreau was cited as one of the main authors of the report. So he did work on Summerland after all. I wonder why he denied it last night.

Boudreau's name was circled in red. Hamish, intrigued, scanned the lists of authors of the other reports. One report, dated after the casino had begun to be built, had two names circled in red also, those of Clarence Chen and John Kamara. The guest list for the party seems to lead back to Summerland. And of course Francis Chastain would have to have been aware about the reports, even if he was not cited as an author. So his retirement party was really a way for Bob to probe the involvement of his guests with the country. I'd better talk to the head of APTI about this.

*****

Hamish introduced himself to Tim Blacket, the current president of APTI, on the phone. "Can I have a few moments of your time? I was at a retirement party for Francis Chastain, hosted by Bob Wismer, and this morning he was found drowned. There are some suspicious circumstances. I know that you commissioned Bob to write a history of APTI, and relations with Summerland would have been a focus of the book he was writing. It also was a topic of discussion at the party, and I think that the guest list was chosen from those who worked on that country for APTI."

Blacket was a Canadian with a background at Global Affairs, who had not previously worked at APTI before being named as its head but had extensive experience working in African countries. "Sure, we had a discussion about that. I told him I thought he needed to shed light on why Summerland turned out the way it did. But I didn't want it to become public knowledge that he was looking into it. It might come to nothing. So you're saying his death is suspicious?"

"Well, at the moment the police think that it was an accident, but I'm not so sure. I'm planning on sticking around here for a few more days and looking into it. Can I get your permission to approach current or former staff to ask about Summerland?"

"How about taking over from Bob in writing a history of APTI?"

"I wouldn't be able to work on it full time, since I have other cases to deal with. It would probably involve a lot of travel away from Nova Scotia to interview people in the various countries APTI dealt with. I could see this taking me a number of years. "

"Well, think it over. In the meantime you could use it as a cover for your questions about Summerland, if you are investigating a possible link with Bob's death."

"Great, thanks. I'll be in touch if I learn anything useful. And I'll think about your offer."

OTTAWA AND GATINEAU, SEPT. 18

Hamish got out of his rental car and rang the doorbell of the bungalow in Manor Park. He had obtained the address of Terence Deaver's widow from the personnel department of APTI. A grey-haired woman who looked to be in her 70s answered the door, giving Hamish a smile. "Hi, I'm Angela, come on in, Hamish. After your call, I dug out Terence's papers. I'd been wondering what to do with them. Have a look, and take away the ones you want. You said you might be writing a history of the place, so it would make sense for you to keep them."

"Did he ever talk about Summerland? He must have been going there a lot in the 1990s."

"You're right, he was. But it was so long ago, so I can't tell you much. I do remember that he told me about elaborate dinners that they offered him there. He was meeting with the president and his cabinet ministers. He came back once with a monstrous pearl. It was so large I didn't even try to get it set into a brooch or necklace. I just keep it in my safety deposit box."

Hamish sat down at the desk where Angela had left the papers. There were official documents as well as handwritten notes, and a diary with entries indicating travel dates and appointments. He called to Angela: "Is it really all right if I take all of this away? It's too much for me to go through here. After I'm done I can leave it with the archivist at APTI, and she can decide what's worth keeping."

"Sure, that will be fine. Let me give you a box to put them in."

Hamish took the box back to the cottage, and laid its contents on the dining room table, next to the accordion file containing Bob's material on Summerland. He had alerted Bob's executor to his desire to stay there a few more days, and the latter gave his approval. "There's a key underneath the mat at the front door. Just lock up when you leave, but give me a heads up so I'll know when the place will be empty."

Hamish first compared the two sets of official papers–Bob's and Terence's. They were mostly the same, but in some cases the latter were drafts, not the final official documents. Intrigued, he looked through Terence's draft paper giving APTI's decision on the casino. Dated January 23, 1994, it was considerably more positive on the advantages of a casino for generating government revenue and attracting tourism than the final version of March 15, 1994. It did not state that APTI would refuse to provide technical assistance on its implementation. The draft cited Terence Deaver as one of the authors, while the final copy did not. *Hmm, it seems that Terence disagreed with the final report. I wonder what he did about it.*

After March, 1994, neither set included further papers dealing with Summerland that had Terence's name on it. Hamish glanced through the diary to see if Terence's work on the country had stopped. He saw a number of entries in February-March that said: "meet with F." He gathered that this meant that he had frequent meetings with Francis Chastain. This continued into April-May. There were entries for flight reservations, giving an airline code and a flight number. It should be easy to track down the destination of the flight, to see if he was visiting Summerland.

Hamish decided to contact Chastain to get more background, and gave him a call. "Would you mind very much if I came to talk to you about Summerland? I've spoken to Tim Blacket, and he wants me to take over from Bob in writing a history of APTI. I haven't said yes, I've just promised to think it over."

"Right-o. Do you want to come by this afternoon at 2 or so? I'm at my cottage now." He gave Hamish directions.

It was only just about noon so Hamish went back to the files to see if there were other issues that he should raise with Francis. The diary listed a number of names with whom Terence was scheduled to have meetings. He wondered if they had taken place in Summerland, and again he judged that it shouldn't be too hard to establish whether they were or not.

After fixing himself a sandwich, Hamish checked on Google Maps the route to Chastain's cottage. He realised now that it was just a two kilometre drive north, along the Gatineau River, on the same winding road as Wismer's. I wonder if Francis went back to Ottawa the night before last, or instead just drove to his cottage.

He threw the two files, Deaver's and Wismer's, into the trunk of the car, in case he needed to refer to them when he saw Chastain, and set off.

*****

The cottage owned by Francis Chastain was considerably grander than Bob's. A semi-circular driveway led from the road to the front door, which was flanked by a pair of floor-to-ceiling Palladian windows. Curious, Hamish walked around the side of the house to savour the view up and down the river. There were large bay windows at the back of the house. Double glass doors opened up onto a cantilevered deck, made of large roughly-hewn square timbers, projecting over the slope. The deck was surrounded by waist-high glass railings. This must have cost a small fortune. What a view of the river!

Hamish rang the bell at the front door, half expecting a butler to answer it. Instead, Francis greeted him and led him out to the deck. "Can I get you something to drink? Perhaps a gin and tonic?"

Hamish declined politely. After chatting about his happy memories of working for APTI, he got to the point of his visit. "I glanced through a file in Bob's cottage and noticed that at least three of the guests had worked on Summerland. Their names were on official papers prepared at APTI. Bob had circled their names, which suggests to me that they were invited to the party for their connection to Summerland. Yet each of them denied any knowledge of the casino, and pretended not to have worked on the country at all. Why was that, do you think? I'd ask them myself, but I'm the only one left at the cottage."

Francis looked startled, and took a moment before answering. He shook his head. "I have no idea! I was surprised by the guest list, since I don't know any of them well. I've lost touch with most of the people who were there, except for Bob and Clarence."

"Sorry to raise this, but wouldn't you have been consulted about the casino question at the time, and had meetings with those involved? After all, as head of the legal department you would have to have signed off on the reply to the Summerland authorities."

"It's true, I do remember those discussions, but they were with a large group drawn from APTI's various departments, and not necessarily people with whom I worked from day to day." Francis looked tired. "Anyway, that was a long time ago. Sometimes I think that my mind is a fallow pasture, where my shrivelled memories go to graze! I can't recall much of what happened twenty years ago anymore."

Hamish looked out over the water below, where there was a well-built dock with what looked like a Boston Whaler skiff with a large outboard motor. Beside it, a woman was swimming in the river. She got onto the dock using the swim ladder. She was wearing a pink bikini, which showed off her long legs, narrow waist, and ample breasts. She had a honey-coloured tan on her whole body. She waved to Francis.

"My wife," he said. "She likes to swim, and soon it will be too chilly."

Tearing his attention away from the woman, Hamish turned the other way and motioned with his head: "It must be nice to boat along the river? How far up can you go?"

"There's a dam upriver, but one can still go a few kilometres north from here, anyway. But in the spring, you have to be especially careful to spot the deadheads, logs cut during the winter and left on the ice that became water-logged before they had a chance to float downriver to the pulp and paper plant. Almost all of the log is under water. If you hit one with your motor boat, you could punch a hole in its hull. Someone I knew drowned that way. Tell me, have you decided whether to write the history of APTI? You know the new president asked me first, but I declined, so he asked Bob. I have other things I would rather do."

"No, I'll do some more digging first, and see what turns up, then consider whether it's worth devoting a few years of my time writing about APTI. I also have another interest in Summerland, because the daughter of a mining executive has gone back there, and her father wants my detective agency to locate her."

Chastain frowned. "What's she doing there? It's about as dead as Soho on a Sunday morning!"

"She's researching a thesis on the relations between the country and the great powers following the end of the Cold War."

Chastain shook his head: "No use stirring up dying embers. In any case, should you need to consult me again, feel free to call."

Hamish looked again down to the water, where Chastain's wife was towelling herself off on the pontoon. He thought he recognized her, but couldn't figure out how or when they had met.

Chastain walked Hamish back to the front door. "How long are you staying at Bob's cottage?"

"Another few days. I'll book my return when I'm ready to give Blacket my answer on writing the history. Oh, another question I forgot to ask you: Terence Deaver has entries in his diary in the weeks before the paper on the casino was finalized, with the notation 'Meet with F'. Do you remember meeting with him then? I gather he was more favourable to the casino than the rest of the staff."

Chastain paused on the sill. "Just the letter F, was it? It wouldn't have been me. I can't think of another person with that initial who worked at APTI at the time, but who knows, there were a few hundred employees. And it was a long time ago." He shrugged dismissively, then stuck out his hand to say goodbye.

GATINEAU AND ASHCROFT, SEPT. 18-19

"Is that Jessica Bowles? This is Hamish Cameron, I'm still at Bob's cottage. Can I come by to talk to you?"

"Of course, Hamish. Are you free for dinner? I gather that you're on your own, so perhaps we could meet at a restaurant in downtown Gatineau. How about the Sans Façon at 7 pm?"

Hamish entered the restaurant and looked around for Jessica. He was a few minutes late, having taken a detour to avoid construction and only with difficulty had located the address. He spotted her at a table for two across the room, and she waved to him.

She was an attractive woman in her 60s who was neatly dressed and immaculately coiffed, her layered grey-blonde hair hanging down to her shoulders. She smiled at him. "Hamish, please sit down. It's terrible about Bob's tragic death. He was a good friend of mine once, after my husband and I divorced fifteen years ago, though I hadn't seen him for some time until the party. How about you: did you know him well?"

"Actually no, though we've kept in touch over the years since I left Ottawa. I'd called him because I wanted to find out about Summerland. I'm trying to locate a young woman who has gone there recently. That was when Bob invited me to the party. A curious thing, though: I think that the guest list was chosen from people who had worked on Summerland at around the time the casino project was floated. He'd circled the names of authors of studies done at APTI at that time, and they included at least three of those who were guests the night before last. But the striking thing was, when Bob brought up the budget allocated to Ocean Pearl, everyone there denied having been involved!"

"Yes, that was curious. And I was also struck by the fact that Francis didn't want to talk about it. He clearly wants to forget the whole thing."

A waiter came over to take their dinner orders. Hamish quickly scanned the menu and noted that despite the restaurant's name, the food was very fancy, with prices to match. He ordered a seafood risotto and a glass of white wine, while Jessica chose a halibut steak.

Hamish turned back to Jessica. "What about you? Did you also get involved in discussions of the Summerland casino? You said you were wholly occupied with the negotiations taking place in South Africa at the time."

"I was only peripherally involved with the Summerland work. I commented on what other people wrote. I have no direct knowledge of the country nor do I have a legal background."

"So, do you think I should write this history of APTI that Tim Blacket wants me to take over from Bob?"

"If I were you, I'd leave it alone. Finding out the real truth about Summerland would take a lot of digging, not to mention the work in researching and writing about APTI's involvement in other countries going back to the late 1950s."

The waiter came back with their entrees, so they stopped talking in order to enjoy their food. After a few minutes Hamish returned to the subject. "Upon reflection, I'm going to agree with you. I've got too much to do, and I'm not well placed to write this history. I'm neither someone with much inside knowledge nor an impartial observer who can be outspoken in his criticism."

"Well, I'm sure Tim will be disappointed. He's my former husband, by the way. He heard a lot about APTI from me years ago, and complained that I was spending so much time working for them in Africa that I was a WINO–a Wife in Name Only! We drifted apart, and decided there was nothing left in our relationship. Now that I work in Global Affairs I do a lot less travelling, though I'm responsible for Canada's relations with several African countries."

Hamish was reminded of how close-knit Ottawa was. Most people worked for the government, and everyone knew everyone else, or knew someone who did. They rubbed shoulders at parties, at the Rec Centre, or at the Britannia Yacht Club. There were few secrets that could remain so for long.

Jessica continued: "What about you, Hamish? I gather you were a judge until you reached retirement age."

"My second career as a detective happened by accident. I was in an upscale retirement home because I didn't want to handle domestic chores and wanted companionship. I noticed some funny things going on, and with the help of a volunteer at the residence, Sean Carroll, we brought the bad guys to justice. When others in town heard about it they came to us with their own issues they wanted us to investigate, so we decided to go into business together."

"Who's this young woman you're looking for in Summerland?"

"She's Amelia Armbrister, the daughter of Kevin Armbrister, a mining executive. That reminds me, who can I talk to at Global Affairs who could advise me how to go about locating her? Do we even have an embassy there?"

"No, just a consulate. It does routine work such as interviewing visa applicants and serving as a point of contact for the few Canadians still living there. As I recall, at one stage there was a major Canadian mining operation, but that was closed down years ago. I'll give you the contact information for the consulate." She emptied her glass and got ready to go. "Oh, and before I forget, here is a print of the photograph I took at Bob's party."

Hamish drove back to the cottage, determined now to book a flight back to Halifax the next day. As he turned off the forest road toward Bob's house, he was shocked to see that there were flames visible through the windows. The whole of the ground floor seemed to be engulfed in fire. He slammed on the brakes, grabbed his phone, and called 911. "Envoyez les pompiers! Vite!"

He approached the house to see if he could salvage his suitcase and clothes, but the heat was intense and he didn't dare go through the front door. The lack of oxygen made him pant, and he hurriedly retreated to his car. As he waited for the fire truck he watched flames inside start to lick at the windows on the upper level. After another fifteen minutes, a fire truck hurtled into the driveway, siren wailing. Mounting the truck's ladder while pulling up the hose, a fireman poked it through a second story window and poured water into the house. Soon, the flames had been extinguished, but the cottage was now a hollowed-out building, whose contents had been either consumed by the flames or soaked in water.

It's a good thing I kept the Summerland files in the trunk of my car, Hamish thought.

*****

Hamish woke up in the hotel room he had rented after being told that he should stay put in order to be interviewed the next day. He drove to the Gatineau police station on Boulevard Gréber, then spent most of the morning there speaking to the police and the fire inspector. The cottage was a write-off. They were investigating whether arson was involved.

Inspecteur Giroux stared at him suspiciously when Hamish explained that he had left no lights or appliances on before leaving for dinner. "So you have no idea what caused the fire? I should warn you that my boss now thinks Monsieur Vismère's death might not be an accident, so we're going to be looking very, very carefully at all the evidence. I'm waiting for the DNA analysis of the stains on the rock we found. As of now, you are not to leave the country."

He arrived back in Halifax late in the evening with just the clothes on his back and the files on Summerland. His suitcase had disappeared in the fire. Hamish retrieved his car from the airport parking lot and returned to The Oaks, looking forward to being able to take a shower and change his clothes.

"What a trip!" he told Sean. "I didn't learn much about Summerland, and now I can't travel there, since I've been ordered to stay in Canada! So if Armbrister insists that someone go find his daughter there, it will have to be you."

"He called me again today. He said that if we don't get cracking he won't pay us another cent. He sounded mad, and anxious about his daughter. I told him that the phones were still down in Summerland, but I would try again to contact her. I guess I'd better book plane reservations. There's only one flight a week to Balabo and back, from Cairo on Wednesdays. I'm looking forward to the change of scene anyway. I keep feeling that I'm just treading water here."

BALABO,
SEPTEMBER 21-22

Sean got off the Air Summerland flight in a daze, made worse by the moist early evening air and a temperature of 35 C. He had hardly slept on the flight to London, and though he had dozed off while awaiting the departure to Frankfurt from Heathrow, his body clock had kept him awake during that flight and the Lufthansa one from Frankfurt to Cairo. By the time the DC3 landed in Balabo after a stop in Khartoum he had been travelling for 24 hours.

The few other passengers, who seemed to be residents, trickled off to their various destinations, and Sean was alone outside the terminal. He hailed the one taxi in the queue. "The Hotel Belvedere, please." The driver just nodded to him, and put the ageing Peugeot 403 in gear.

The Belvedere was the only hotel in town that was still open. It was a relic of the Italian era, with an ornate facade and a shabby interior. The front desk was deserted. Sean rang the bell and waited. After a few minutes, he impatiently slammed the bell with his fist. A lean man wearing dress trousers and a white shirt but no tie came through a door, yawning. "Passport, please." He looked it over, then pocketed it.

Sean protested. "I need my passport back. I can't afford to lose it!"

"We keep. Government regulations. Return it at checkout." He gave Sean a key with a large triangular brass tag with 204 stamped on it. "When you go out, leave it at desk." He nodded to a rack with hooks, most of them occupied with keys. The man turned and walked back through the door the way he had come.

Sean was too weary to call him back to ask about a restaurant and directions for finding his way to the room. He wandered around the ground floor, found a set of stairs, and decided to try the second floor. When he finally located 204 and got the key to turn in the lock, he entered and collapsed on the bed. In a minute, he was asleep.

The sun pouring in through the window woke Sean at six. He felt better after 12 hours of sleep, though he was badly in need of food. He decided not to change out of his wrinkled clothes. Instead, he went down the stairs to the still deserted lobby, and rang the bell. After only a minute the same man as the previous night came to the desk. Sean decided that he must be on duty 24 hours of the day.

"Can you tell me if there's a restaurant where I can get breakfast? Is there one here at the hotel?"

"Yes, floor number eight. Elevator at back of lobby." He pointed at a small door which Sean had not noticed before that was in the corner of the ground floor diagonally opposite to the entrance doors.

Sean entered the cage, slid the folding grille back in place, and pressed a button with the numeral 8. Nothing happened. Sean was about to get out to return to the desk when the cage lurched into motion. After 7 bumps and crashes it stopped suddenly. Sean slid open the grille, pushed the door outward, and entered a vast room crowded with tables. Only two were occupied, one by a couple who looked like European tourists, and another by a man with Chinese features. Uncertain of where to sit, Sean hesitated, then picked a small table near a window that gave a panoramic view of downtown Balabo.

A man wandered over with a pad of paper in hand. He said something that Sean didn't understand.

"Do you understand English? What do you have for breakfast?"

The man shook his head. He started making gestures, making a circle with his thumb and forefinger, and cupping his hands.

Sean shrugged his shoulders, then nodded his head. "I'll have whatever it is."

The man nodded, seemingly understanding that Sean was resigned to eating the food that was on offer. He re-emerged twenty minutes later holding a tray, upon which was a poached egg and a cup with liquid that looked to Sean like black sludge. Two slices of hard bread were accompanied by a serving dish of orange slime.

Sean spread the slime, which he hoped was jam, on the bread and bit into it gingerly. The bread was softer than it looked, and the jam was tasty. He thought, this must be mango. Not bad!

The coffee was strong but very sweet. In a few minutes Sean had wolfed down the egg and bread, and emptied the cup except for the coffee grounds at the bottom. He looked around for the waiter to ask for more.

The man emerged with another tray, containing exactly the same things as the first one.

Sean, eating more slowly this time, finished this one off too. When the waiter returned, looking inquiringly, Sean waved his hands horizontally in the seemingly universal signal that he had had enough.

*****

At the front desk, Sean showed a photo of Amelia and asked whether she had stayed at the hotel. The man squinted at the photo, turning it sideways and frowning.

"She stay here, yes, two weeks ago."

"Can you find out where she is now?"

He appeared not to understand.

Sean reached into his pocket, and took out his wallet. He had changed $500 into Summerland dinars in Cairo, and was given a handful of notes of various sizes. He chose one of the larger notes, without knowing its value but assuming that it must represent a substantial sum. He put it on the counter. "Do you know where she is?"

The man said. "Maybe," as he slid the bill off the counter and palmed it. "Try Mustafa at the news kiosk down the street." He pointed to the left.

Sean walked out into the mid-morning sun, feeling the pall of hot humid air settle over him. He was annoyed with himself for not having brought a hat, a good pair of sunglasses, and some sunscreen. He was going to have to try to buy them. He walked down the street in the direction of the kiosk, which he could see 100 metres away. It was a small wooden hut, with a counter about a metre wide and a man sitting behind it. Various newspapers were displayed on wire racks in front of it. Sean noted two-or-three-day-old copies of the Times of London, le Monde, Corriere della Sera, and Frankfurter Zeitung. There were also newspapers in Arabic of unknown provenance, at least to Sean.

"Are you Mustafa?" When the man nodded his head, Sean continued: "I'm looking for a young woman from Canada, named Amelia. Would you happen to know where she is?"

Mustafa looked dubious, so Sean took out another bank note and held it in his hand, keeping it well away from the other man. "I'll give you money if you take me to her."

"I can show you." He reached for the bill, but Sean pulled it back and thrust it into the pocket of his trousers.

"Not until you show me where she is. Is it far?"

"Not so far." Mustafa pulled the wire racks into the hut and closed the door above the counter, putting a padlock on the hasp. "Come with me." He led Sean down an alley toward a complex of buildings, each about 10 stories tall, and seemingly a few decades old.

Sean saw a large sign in front of one of the buildings as they approached it that said National University of Summerland, below an inscription in Arabic.

Turning to the right, Mustafa led Sean into what appeared to be a university residence. "Woman you want is living here." He put out his hand, but Sean shook his head.

"You need to take me to her. I have no idea how to go about finding her here."

Mustafa shrugged his shoulders. He walked to the back of the lobby, opened the door to an office, and ushered Sean inside. A woman wearing a niqab was seated behind a desk, on which was placed a CRT monitor. She was staring at the flickering screen, but looked up as they entered. After Mustafa spoke to her in Arabic for several minutes, she turned to Sean and said in very good English:

"I understand that you are looking for North American woman. We have an Amelia Armbrister staying here. She is doing research at the university. If you leave me your name I will ask her to contact you at the Hotel Belvedere."

Though Sean would have liked to have waited for Amelia, he nodded his head, thanked the woman, and gave Mustafa his tip. On the way back, Mustafa pointed out a store where he could buy some tourist necessities. Sean also noted that there was a restaurant next to the university that posted menus in English, French, and German that included meat and fish dishes. He decided to try it for dinner.

BALABO, SEPTEMBER 23-24

When he got back from an early dinner Sean found a note in the pigeon hole beside his key in the rack by the front desk. It read: "I'm guessing you were sent by my father to find me. Come to the lobby of my building tomorrow morning at 9. Amelia Armbrister."

After one serving of the same breakfast as the day before, Sean returned to the residence for women students. In the lobby was a young woman wearing a hijab covering her face and a grey robe down to her feet. Sean went over to her and said with a smile, "Amelia, I presume?"

She nodded. "Good of you to come. Let me explain: I haven't been hiding from my father but I haven't made any effort to contact him either. In any case, the cell phone I purchased here only seems to work for domestic calls. It may just be that the regime doesn't approve of contacts with the outside world." Sean could see the twinkle in the eyes peering over the mask on her face.

"So, how long do you intend to stay? Are you making progress on your research? I think your father will want to come here to fetch you if you don't return to Canada soon."

"So far I haven't been able to talk to anyone important. Maybe it's just a wild goose chase. There's one person that I remember from my time here, who used to work for my father. He was in charge of the political aspects of opening a mine, getting government approvals and negotiating royalty rates–that sort of thing. He was always very nice to me, and even sent me birthday cards when I was back in Canada. But after a few years, he stopped. I'm trying to locate him again but so far, no luck."

"Perhaps I can help you find him. I'm booked on the next weekly flight to Cairo, so I still have four days to kill here. It might be easier for a man to ask questions than for you as a woman. I'm sure your father will cover my expenses."

"Sounds good. I suggest you try the Ministry of Natural Resources or whatever it's called here. See if they know of a man called Mukhtaar Hassan. I'll write it down for you. I suspect he is still working in the mining business in some capacity. I'm going to wander around my old neighbourhood, to see if there is someone there who remembers my family."

Sean went back to the hotel and asked the man at the desk for the location of the Ministry of Natural Resources. He felt lost not being able to access the internet.

The man looked puzzled. "Natural Resources?"

"You know, oil, lithium deposits, iron ore ..."

"Oh, you mean the Mining Commission! What do you want with them?" He frowned.

"I'm just trying to locate someone. A friend."

The man pointed in the direction opposite to the university. "Low lying building with picture of a gold nugget on the sign. About 1 kilometre."

The building looked like a warehouse because there were few windows. He walked up the steps to what seemed to be the main entrance door. A man in a light brown uniform stopped him, and asked him a question that he did not understand. Sean noticed a reception desk further inside, and pointed to it. The other made a gesture that he should stay where he was, and went over to a chair next to the wall and picked up a wand. He proceeded to wave it up and down Sean's body. Finding nothing, he motioned for Sean to go to the reception.

A middle-aged man with a lined face behind the counter stared at Sean as he approached.

"Do you speak English? I'm looking for someone called Mukhtaar Hassan. Can you tell me if he works here?" Sean showed him the piece of paper Amelia had given him.

The man shook his head. "Not here," he said.

"Have you heard of him? Where could I find him?"

He shrugged his shoulders, and went back to sorting through papers on his desk.

Sean had no choice but to retreat. As he left, he looked around. A group of men were coming down the hall that led to the main entrance. Among them he thought he recognized the Chinese looking man he had seen at breakfast the day before.

Back at the hotel, Sean went over to the front desk, behind which stood his friend. He took out another bill, but smaller this time.

"How can I find someone called Mukhtaar Hassan? Is there a phone directory? Can I call telephone information?" He placed the bill on the counter, but kept his fist on it.

"Directory very old. Not reliable. But I look." He went back through the door behind the front desk.

He came out a few minutes later holding a piece of paper, which he waved in Sean's face.

"Listings for Mukhtaar Hassan who live in Balabo in old directory." He ran his finger down a list of half a dozen names and addresses. "Common name."

"So how do I find these people?" Sean said with discouragement in his voice.

"I can sell you a map for 25 dinars."

Sean looked down at the bill on the counter, seeing that its denomination was 10 dinars. With a sigh, he rummaged through his wallet to find the additional 15, and gave the bills to him.

Sean went over to a sofa in the lobby and spread the map out on a low table in front of him. Starting with the Mukhtaar Hassan at the top of the list, he tried to locate his address on the map. The writing was small, and he wasn't sure about the abbreviations since they were not the standard St., Ave., or Blvd.

He went back to the desk. "What does B. stand for?"

"Barabara. It means street in Swahili."

Sean went back to the sofa, but he could not locate the barabara in the first listing on the map, so he gave up and went back to the desk. "Would you please find the addresses on the map and circle them?"

The man didn't say anything but looked at him quizzically.

Sean took a bill from his wallet and displayed it. "Is this enough?"

The man put up two fingers, so Sean took out another bill of the same denomination. His stock of cash was getting depleted. *I sure hope there are money changers who will exchange my Canadian cash into dinars.* He waited by the desk as the man circled the locations on the map, identifying each one by a number that corresponded to its position on the list.

*****

Sean and Amelia had agreed to meet for lunch at a university restaurant near her residence that was reasonably priced.

"The buffet's not bad at lunch time," Amelia said.

"I'll have the same." Sean tried small amounts of each of the dishes and ended up liking the curried chicken best. He felt comfortable talking to Amelia. She had a straightforward manner, neither aggressive nor flirty. She had a ready smile when something amused her, and she seemed to enjoy Sean's company.

"So how did you make out, Amelia? Has your old neighbourhood changed a lot?"

"Fortunately the buildings are still pretty much the way they were when I lived here. I located my house without much trouble. The family who used to be our neighbours on one side is no longer there, but on the other side the woman remembered me. When I asked her about Mukhtaar Hassan, she couldn't or wouldn't tell me where he was. She claimed not to know him, though I'm sure I remember that they talked to each other when I was here before. So I struck out. What about you?"

Sean showed her the list of those with the name Mukhtaar Hassan and the map with the half dozen circles. "Here are the locations of men with that name in the old phone directory. Two of them seem to be within about a kilometre of here. Do you want to try those first? I wouldn't recognize the man you knew, nor do I know enough Swahili to make myself understood."

"I only know a few words myself. But if we stumble upon the right house, the family should know some English."

After their meal they walked through the dusty streets of one- and two-story homes to the nearest one on the list, a modest house made of stone and mud. A woman answered the door. Amelia bid her good afternoon: "*Habari ya Alasiri.*" Then she said: "Do you speak English? I am looking for a Mukhtaar Hassan I knew long ago. Does he live here?"

The woman shook her head. "*Hapana,*" she said, then went back into her house.

The second house was somewhat nicer, as were the other houses on this street. Sean thought, *this looks more promising.*

A woman answered the door. As before, Amelia gave a greeting in Swahili and then switched to English. This time, the woman answered in fluent, though accented, English.

"Who is this man Mukhtaar Hassan, and why do you want to talk to him?"

"He worked for my father's company, Truro Resources, when I lived here about 20 years ago. He was a friend of mine."

The woman frowned. "There are no more foreign companies here. It's not good to dig up memories of that time. I cannot help you." She quickly went inside, after looking around carefully to see if anyone was watching them. She closed the door and they could hear the bolt being pushed home.

"This isn't going very well. I have the feeling that the woman here knows my Mukhtaar Hassan, but doesn't want to admit it. We could try the others on the list, but I doubt we'd have any luck."

"What do you want to do now? Maybe it's a good time to call it quits and go back to Canada," Sean said hopefully.

As they walked back to the hotel, Sean had the feeling someone was watching them. The street was not very busy, as Balabo did not seem to offer much in the way of employment or shopping. He made a gesture to Amelia, and stopped to look into the window of a dingy shop that sold men's clothing. He looked back the way they had come and noticed a man dressed in Western clothes who was walking toward them, but looking nonchalantly around, not at them. He passed by and continued on his course, turning right at the next cross street. *I guess I was imagining things.* To Amelia, he said: "I just want to look in here for a hat to protect me from the sun."

Sean emerged a few minutes later with what looked like a safari hat. "All I need now is an elephant gun and I could pass for a big game hunter! At least it will keep the sun out of my face."

Amelia said in a determined voice: "To get back to your question, I still want to talk to people at the university, to do some research before I go back to Canada. I'll let you know in a day or two if I can get enough done in time to take the same flight as you to Cairo."

ASHCROFT, SEPTEMBER 25

Hamish had promised to get back to Tim Blacket with a decision on whether to write the history of APTI. He unpacked the files he had taken back from Ottawa, the files he had put into his rental car before Bob Wismer's cottage went up in smoke. *I'll have one last look at these to see if I missed any clues.*

Again he kept Bob's files and Terry's in separate piles. He scratched his head. *Why are there two versions of these papers? And how can there be a separate budget allocation that was not approved by the board?* Then he remembered that there were ad hoc funds contributed by individual countries that were run separately from the main budget. For instance, one of the former colonial powers might want their contributions to be directed to a particular country with which they retained close relations.

The countries with former ties to Summerland were Italy, then France and Britain. Could one of them have financed a feasibility study for the casino? The first two seemed unlikely. Britain was less certain. *I'll need to talk to Francis Chastain again.*

Hamish looked through Terence Deaver's files. The papers there, unlike Bob Wismer's, did not cite as contributors Roger Boudreau, Clarence Chen, or John Kamara. So their involvement with Summerland seemed to have stopped by the time work on the casino began.

While he was thinking through the next steps to take, the office phone rang. It was Kevin Armbrister. "What have you found out about my daughter? I haven't received a word from Sean Carroll, nor from Amelia! If you can't get me any information about them, I'm going to fly to Balabo myself!"

"I don't think that would be wise. I'm sure Sean would have contacted us if he could. I believe that there are no outgoing calls from Summerland to Canada, at least not from mobile phones. I'll try again to contact the hotel where he's staying. I'll let you know if I learn anything." He said goodbye and hung up.

*****

The call to Francis Chastain went to voicemail. Hamish left a message requesting a call back, but he suspected that he would not get one. I think he's deliberately avoiding talking to me about Summerland, especially since he knows I might be writing about it.

Hamish put in a call to Tim Blacket, whose secretary put him through right away. "Tim, I'm still trying to understand what went on with Summerland, but I think I know why there was an allocation of money for work on the casino even though the board had refused to get involved. I'll bet that this was done through one of the country funds. Would you have records of those going back to the mid-1990s? Could you find out which country financed it?"

"Sure Hamish, I'll get someone to have a look, and let you know. Are you any closer to a decision on writing a book about APTI?"

"No, not until I get a better idea about what there is to write about Summerland. By the way, why are you so keen on publishing this history?"

"Well, I keep getting signals from board members that their governments may pull the plug on us, so I'd like there to leave a record of what the organization did."

*****

Since his calls could not go through to Summerland, Hamish tried sending a telegram to the Hotel Belvedere. "Attention Sean Carroll. Armbrister demands feedback. Please confirm your arrival and progress in locating Amelia. Hamish."

A few hours later came a reply. "Have arrived safely and located Amelia. She may return with me on Wednesday if she completes her research. Sean." Hamish passed the information on to Armbrister, who promised to stay put pending further news.

BALABO,
SEPTEMBER 26

Sean had little to do now that they had given up on finding Mukhtaar Hassan. He decided to do some tourism before meeting Amelia again for dinner. He had brought with him an old travel guide to the city, and he walked around the old town, which was located close to the port. Balabo was a city of about a hundred thousand people living in low-rise stone or mud buildings, punctuated here and there by sharp-spired mosques. The old town was a jumble of narrow streets and curved arches leading to arcades with shops and hawkers' stalls.

Sean followed the guidebook's directions down a series of alleys toward the city's oldest building, a customs house dating back to the 16th century built by Arab traders. The alleys narrowed. In order to proceed, Sean had to duck his head under an arch where two people could barely pass each other without touching. There were only a few other pedestrians there, and no bicycles, much less cars. Sean began to wonder if he had taken the right route. Perhaps I should have stayed on the main street, where there were crowds of people. The directions in the guidebook may be out of date.

He looked around, thinking that he had heard footsteps. Nobody there. He kept going. The sun did not shine down into the alley, and he couldn't see any light up ahead. This looks like a dead end.

As he was about to head back the way he had come, he felt a hand on his arm. Turning sharply, he saw a tall man in native dress standing in an entryway, beckoning him inside. The man put a finger to his lips. Sean hesitated, then given the man's urgent gesture to follow him, cautiously entered the low hallway that led to an atrium with a fountain.

The man was about Sean's age, though leaner and harder. His hair was covered by a turban, and he wore a macawiis, a long piece of cloth wrapped around his waist. "I am Mukhtaar Hassan. You were looking for me?" he asked in fluent English.

"Glad to meet you! I was looking for you on behalf of Amelia Armbrister, who wants to talk to you. Do you remember her?"

"Ah, Amelia. Yes, I remember the Armbristers very well, since I worked for her father. She was such an amusing child." He rubbed the stubble on his chin. "So why does she want to talk to me?"

Sean was still wary. "How did you know I was with her? And how did you happen to be in the same place I was walking?"

The man laughed. "Everyone knows who you are, and who Amelia Armbrister is. There are so few foreigners here, you stand out like goats in a field of sheep! I saw you leave your hotel, with a guide book in your hand. I knew you would take this route to the old customs house, since that's the main tourist attraction in the old town. So you would have to pass by at some point."

Sean was now convinced of the man's bona fides. "Very well, Amelia is working on an academic thesis on Summerland. She wants to understand the influence of the great powers on the politics here."

"We're not allowed to discuss politics with foreigners. If the government knew I even spoke to you I could go to jail. I'm already in enough trouble thanks to your visit to the Mining Commission. And you are in danger too."

"She just wants some general knowledge of what happened to tip the country from the influence of the Western governments into the orbit of China."

"And she comes to me? What is it that she thinks I know?" He looked suspiciously at Sean.

"She also wants to see you, because you were kind when she lived here as a child."

"Well, she's asking dangerous questions. I know nothing, though like everyone here, I have my suspicions. But even talking about it can get both me and Amelia in trouble. Best just leave it alone, go back to Canada, and forget it!"

Hassan stopped and listened, then pushed Sean behind a curtain. A man was outside, the noise of his footsteps barely perceptible because it was muffled by his slippers. He stuck his head through the open entryway. He looked around the atrium. Seeing nothing, he retreated and continued on his way.

Sean let out a sigh of relief. Though sceptical before, he was now convinced of the danger he was in. "I'll make sure both Amelia and I get out of the country as soon as possible. We're scheduled to fly out to Cairo in two days. But I'm sure that Amelia would want to see you before she leaves. Can you at least do that? I'm meeting her for lunch tomorrow."

Hassan stroked his chin and frowned. "Maybe I can arrange something. Where are you two meeting? I'll try to be on your path back to the residence where she is staying. I'll at least be able to exchange a few words with her then."

Hassan accompanied Sean on his route toward the customs house. "You should be safe after you get there, the streets are wider and there are more people. But go back to your hotel by the main boulevard and avoid the alleyways."

The customs building was unremarkable, constructed of mud and squared off timbers. There was a caretaker who offered to give Sean a tour, but in a language he didn't understand. A plaque explained in several languages the history of the building and its significance in the trade relations with neighbouring countries.

On his way back to the hotel, Sean came across a large dilapidated concrete structure that loomed over neighbouring vacant lots. On its roof was a sign that read "Ocean Pearl Casino." It was deserted, with a sheet of plywood nailed across its main entrance. Graffiti adorned its walls, and the parking lot which was once no doubt occupied by fancy cars owned by its patrons was now covered in weeds and scattered trash. A nearby building appeared to be a hotel, but it was closed. It was similarly boarded up.

Sean poked his foot into a pile of rubbish, uncovering a round plastic token. *It looks like a gambling chip.* On one side was the inscription "Ocean Pearl, 10 dollars." The other side had Chinese characters. *I'll keep this as a souvenir.*

BALABO, SEPTEMBER 27-28

Sean and Amelia walked back slowly to her residence after eating lunch. She told Sean that she had talked to a few university students there, but had not been able to learn much about the current state of politics in the country. The military government took instructions from the clerics, who demanded that priority be given to studying the Koran. Western subjects like international relations were tolerated, at least for the moment, but there were rumours that a crackdown was imminent. Women were still able to study at university, but how long that would continue was uncertain.

As they turned a corner leading to her building, a man in native dress approached them. They stepped aside to let him pass, then Sean recognized that it was the man that he had encountered yesterday. Amelia said "Mukhtaar!"

"Yes, it's me, but keep your voice down. I can't be observed talking to you. I need to flee the country; my sources tell me that I'm now a hunted man. I just wanted to see you again before I leave."

Amelia's face fell. "Tell me, what has happened to Summerland, the country that used to be so laid back, so relaxed and happy?"

"It's become a strict Islamic state where everything related to Western values is banned. We have no liberties, except those reluctantly allowed by the clerics. There is no freedom of speech. We can be arrested for communicating with foreigners, and I have secrets that would be dangerous to the regime."

Two women approached them and Mukhtaar stopped talking. He stuck out his hand as if to ask Sean and Amelia for alms. When the women had passed, he said: "I can't stay here any longer. Do you think your father would offer me a job? I can probably make it out to Ethiopia by road, and take a plane from there. But if I try to communicate with him from here the regime will know about it, and that could be the end of me."

"I'll ask him to confirm, but I'm sure he would be happy to offer you a job at his mine in Tanzania. How can we contact you?"

"I have a sat phone which I kept after Truro Resources left the country. I only use it for emergencies. I'll call you when I get out of Summerland."

Hassan touched Amelia's arm affectionately, bowed to the two of them, and disappeared around the corner.

*****

At the hotel, the familiar receptionist at the front desk made eye contact with Sean and pointed to a man sitting in a chair in the lobby. "He is wanting to talk to you."

The man, who was in a suit that resembled a military uniform, though without badges or decorations, seemed to be in his 40s. He glared at Sean, his mouth curled into a sneer. "So, you have been asking questions. That is not allowed here. If you and your compatriot do not leave tomorrow, we will be forced to take measures. You are warned." He got up and stared fixedly at Sean before walking out the front door of the hotel.

Sean went over to talk to the man at the front desk, but the latter turned and went back to his room at the back, refusing to engage with him.

*****

The plane from Balabo to Cairo was about to depart. Sean and Amelia looked nervously at the official who questioned them. He did not show them any courtesy. "Do you have any artefacts with you? Any Summerland currency?" They answered in the negative but the man stared at them suspiciously for a few seconds before stamping their passports. They proceeded to the departure lounge, which was a Spartan room with only a few chairs, some of which were broken. A flight attendant gestured for them to hurry to embark on the DC3, and when they did so, the door slammed shut and the plane started to taxi down the runway.

When the plane was airborne Amelia put her hand on Sean's arm. She sighed with relief. "Whew, I wondered if we would be allowed to leave. I didn't get much information about what happened in Summerland, but at least I did meet Mukhtaar Hassan. If he makes it to Ethiopia he might be willing to give me his insights into what happened in the 1990s."

"Yes, and we can wait in Cairo for him to call us. In the meantime, you should phone your father to confirm that he will offer him a job at the Truro Resources mine in Tanzania. "

OTTAWA AND GATINEAU, SEPT. 28-29

Hamish sat beside Tim Blacket at the conference table, which was piled with records of the country funds, as they were called– the projects which countries financed directly, but carried out with the help of APTI staff. Hamish had taken the elevator up to the eleventh floor of a plain concrete office building located on O'Connor Street in downtown Ottawa. He remembered the nondescript offices from his days working there some two decades before, though at least the office furniture had been updated.

"It's hard to know where to look, since these projects would not be listed in APTI's annual report," Blacket explained. "But my staff assistant went through the whole set of project proposals, and here is the only one that involves Summerland in the mid-1990s. It was funded by the Chinese government." He handed it to Hamish. "You can see that some of those who attended Francis Chastain's retirement party are mentioned in it. And the project's aim was to establish an economic and legal framework for gambling in the country."

"What about Francis himself? Was he running the show? If not, he must at least have given his permission for the legal staff to be involved."

"You would think so. But in my experience Francis doesn't want to talk about events in Summerland. When I asked him a question about our relations with that country, he claimed it was too long ago, that he doesn't have a clear recollection of what went on then. Very convenient for him!"

"I'll want to talk to the others. May I take a copy of the proposal with me? You'll keep the original in the office safe, I assume?"

Blacket nodded. "Be careful, Hamish. I wonder if the fire at Bob Wismer's cottage was aimed at destroying evidence of APTI's involvement with Summerland."

"Any news of the investigation of possible arson and of Bob's death?"

"The Gatineau police haven't communicated with me, nor has anything appeared in the press."

"I think I'll pay a visit to the police officer in charge to see if I can get an update of their progress on the case."

*****

Inspecteur Giroux sat back in his swivel chair, picking idly at his nose. "No, Monsieur Cameronne, the coroner has not yet ruled on the death of Monsieur Vismère. The DNA found on the rock by the river matches his, but there's no other DNA on it. No footprints that could be those of a murderer. But the fire at his cottage was arson, so Vismère's death is suspicious. The coroner's keeping the case open for now."

"I think there may be a link with events in an African country, Summerland, in the 1990s. I've discovered that several of those who were at the party that night had worked in that country for APTI, the institute that Francis Chastain retired from, at the time."

"What? How does this have anything to do with his death or the fire at his cottage? I know you detective guys are into red herrings, *mais, câlice*, this is going too far!"

"Seriously, someone might have wanted to get rid of any evidence of their involvement with the country's casino, which was built with APTI's help." Hamish looked earnestly at the inspector.

He laughed. "Tell me another one! That country is thousands of kilometres away, and from what you say, those events occurred decades ago! You're not seriously thinking I'll believe this?"

Hamish got up and walked away without saying anything. When he reached the door, he turned and said: "I think you're going to live to regret this," and stomped out.

*****

Hamish rang the bell at Francis Chastain's cottage. It was getting late in the season but he guessed that Chastain would want to enjoy the last few warm fall days by the river. He noted that the skiff with the outboard motor was now on a trailer in the driveway, with a tarp over it.

He heard a female voice call to someone else inside. A minute later, a woman opened the door, looking at Hamish quizzically.

Hamish recognized Francis' wife from his previous visit, when she was swimming in the river. Up close, he was even more dazzled by her beauty. Easily thirty years younger than Francis, she was immaculately dressed in a tan pant suit that showed off her narrow waist and décolletage. Around her neck was a thin gold necklace to which was attached a single, very large, pearl, which hung down from the chain and nestled between her breasts. Her beautiful blonde hair, without a trace of grey, was either natural or the result of frequent visits to the hairdresser, or both. Her face looked familiar to Hamish. *I think I must have met her a long time ago. But where?*

Hamish introduced himself and apologized to Mrs. Chastain for stopping by without warning, explaining that he was hoping to chat with her husband.

The woman turned and called out, "Francis, a visitor for you." She did not invite him in but waited with him by the door. Francis descended a circular staircase to the foyer. When he saw Hamish, he frowned. Without offering a greeting or a smile, he said, "What can I do for you, Hamish?"

Hamish still held his former boss in awe, but he could no longer tolerate being fed half-truths about his past activities. "I think it's time that you admitted your involvement with the casino project in Summerland. Tim Blacket has located documents relative to a project entirely funded by China that several staff members of APTI who reported to you worked on. You must have been aware of this, and indeed, you must have authorized their participation. You can't hide any more behind the excuse that you've forgotten because it was so long ago, or that all you did was comment on the work of other departments."

Chastain sighed. "I guess you'd better come in." Turning to his wife, who was still standing at the door, he said, "Dear, we'll be in the library. It may be a while." He led Hamish down the hall to a room with an old oak desk in the middle, and bound volumes in floor-to-ceiling bookcases built into the four walls. He motioned Hamish to a seat in front of the desk, while Francis sat behind it in a swivel chair.

After settling into his straight-backed wooden armchair, which wasn't very comfortable, Hamish assumed the air of a judge–his former vocation–and asked pointedly: "So what actually happened in Summerland?"

Chastain, swallowed, and took a moment before replying.

"The Summerland government of the time–Western-leaning and keen to keep growing at a fast clip–was unhappy with the board's decision not to support the project. They saw the casino as a cheap and easy way to attract investors and get more revenue for the government. So they went to the Chinese, who had recently joined APTI and were flush with money. The casino was to be built by a Chinese company in any case, and financed by a syndicate of investors from Macau, which as you know is now a Chinese territory. All the Summerland government wanted from us was some advice on the legal and financial framework they would need to put in place. So I agreed to loan some of my staff to the project, provided that they could keep doing their other work. The Chinese offered them generous bonuses for working on the framework for the casino."

Hamish sat up. "Wasn't that a violation of the terms of their employment at APTI? We were not supposed to take bribes or compensation from any official or unofficial body. Isn't that right?"

Chastain looked uncomfortable. "It was a grey area. I let it go."

"Who were the staff who were loaned to the project, exactly? I saw the names of Roger Boudreau, Clarence Chen, and John Kamara on some of the documents. Were there others?"

"They were the core group. Terence Deaver provided continuing liaison with the various ministries in Balabo, since he had been involved with Summerland for some time and understood how the bureaucracy worked there."

"So, did everything go according to plan? How long did this work continue?"

"Yes and no. It seemed straightforward at first: we recommended allowing gambling just at the casino, requiring that the casino provide monthly reports on its gambling activities, and levying a 20 percent tax on the casino's revenues. That was the extent of our advice, and we didn't have any further involvement in the project. A year later the casino was finished and it started its operations. It soon became clear that the government wasn't actually in charge. The syndicate that had built and now ran it held the whip hand over Summerland's cabinet. They had feathered the nests of several of the government ministers, who had no reason to sanction them. The government, if it withdrew the casino's licence, would have an enormous public relations problem, given how much it had touted the project in the past. So the casino became a law to itself. It was a success—at least on its own terms—and attracted some more Macau money. The syndicate built a hotel complex beside the casino, and modernized the port so that Saudi princes and Russian oligarchs could dock their super-yachts there. It became a go-to destination for the glitterati. But little of this trickled down to the Summerland citizenry. The staff of the casino was mainly Chinese, and the port was off-limits to ordinary Summerlanders."

"So what happened to trigger the backlash against the casino?"

Chastain hesitated, breaking the fluency of his narrative. "I don't know. I never actually went to the country, I don't have a real sense of what the natives thought."

Hamish was suspicious of the answer. *I don't believe him. And why call them 'natives'? He's still trying to distance himself from the place.* "So when did APTI's involvement with the project end? Was it already over when the revolution started?"

"Yes, we were long gone by then. After all, our work was preparatory to the operation of the casino, and it had been up and running for a few years before the backlash against the regime."

"But Terence Deaver continued to be a desk officer for Summerland for several more years, didn't he? How about the others, did they work on other things in the country?"

"I wouldn't know about that. If they did, it was in another department. The legal department had no further dealings with the country after we completed our report as part of the Chinese-financed project, which lasted only a year." Chastain stared earnestly at Hamish.

Hamish looked away. He did not believe the tale he had been told. Something important is being left out. But I have no evidence that I can confront him with.

"Two last questions. If everything was above board, why did those at the party deny their involvement with Summerland? And what happened to the report?"

Chastain shrugged his shoulders. "Perhaps it was an attempt not to put me on the spot, since Bob had arranged the party in my honour. Certainly the work on Summerland was not something any of us was proud of, considering how it turned out. As for the report, I think only two copies were made, one for the Summerlanders, and one for the Chinese." He got up quickly, and said to Hamish: "If we're done, I'll escort you out."

The woman was sitting in a chair in the living room near the windows giving out over the river. Hamish gave a little bow and said, "Nice to have met you, Mrs. Chastain."

She smiled seductively. "It's Adele, thank you. I wish you a good stay in the Ottawa area, Hamish." She turned back to the book in her lap.

Hamish had an epiphany. Of course! She used to work at APTI.

*****

Hamish told Tim Blacket of his conversation with Francis Chastain. "I think he was still blowing smoke at me. He's modified his story only enough to make it fit with the facts that have emerged since the party, but it doesn't really add up. Was it really considered OK for the legal department to go against the decision of the board not to get involved in the casino project? And was it common for countries to give bonuses to APTI staff to work on their pet projects?"

"Absolutely not! That was contrary to the integrity of the organization, and Chastain would have been sanctioned by the board if they had known of it. I can understand that the staff involved may have been sworn to secrecy. I'll bet that was the real reason that the three men at the party declined to admit their involvement."

"It still doesn't make sense for them to have risked their reputations to prepare a report of the Summerlanders. I think there must have been some major inducement at the time for them to do so. I suppose it's too late to impose penalties on them now, since none of them works for APTI at present?"

"Yes, that's water under the bridge. But Bob's inquiry into those distant events had the potential of tarnishing their reputations, especially that of Francis. Apparently he's angling to get a knighthood in the next Birthday Honours List. A scandal would put paid to that."

"As a British subject and a distinguished international civil servant, I can well imagine that he could hope to receive that honour. As for the others, I guess their loyalty to Francis and concern for their own reputations led them to shut up about it."

"Perhaps. But to change the subject, I gather you met his wife, the lovely Adele. She was actually Bob Wismer's staff assistant at APTI when Francis married her. She was a striking beauty in her mid-twenties then, and she is still gorgeous now. I heard a lot about her from my then-wife Jessica at the time, and about the gifts Francis lavished on her to get her to agree to his marriage proposal."

"It took me a while to figure out where I'd met her before. I hadn't realized that Francis had married her. That certainly was a May-September wedding! I wonder how she likes being married to him, now that he is showing his age."

"Rumour has it that she may have taken up with Bob Wismer, her former boss. After all, their cottages–if you can use that term to describe Francis's place–aren't very far apart. I suspect that she's bored with being Mrs. Chastain, despite the lovely clothes and posh digs."

"That opens up a whole new can of worms concerning the investigation of Bob's death. I've tried suggesting to the Gatineau police that events in Summerland might have some bearing on it and the fire, but Inspecteur Giroux just laughed in my face. Perhaps as head of APTI you can make them take it seriously."

Blacket shook his head. "Let's not jump ahead of ourselves. We don't want to point the finger at Francis until we have something concrete, not just rumours."

"OK, fair enough. I'll continue my digging. I assume I still have your blessing?"

"Go ahead. But please let me know what you find."

CAIRO, OCTOBER 1

Sean and Amelia had booked rooms at the Ramses Hilton. They planned to wait in Cairo until they heard from Mukhtaar, and to do some tourism in the meantime. Their hotel gave a good view of the Nile and of the surrounding sprawl of office buildings, homes, and mosques, the whole giving an exotic ambiance to their stay.

"What about a cruise on a felucca, Amelia? That's a traditional Nile sailboat. I've long wanted to go on one."

They went down to the waterfront and admired the vessels docked there. A child ran up to them. "Hello. Do you want to rent a boat for the day? Just $100 for the two of you, dinner included."

"Sounds good to me. What do you think, Amelia?"

It was a splendid day on the water. The captain and his crew, which consisted only of the ten-year-old named Ahmed who had approached them on the shore, handled the sails as they lazily made their way down the river. There was a gentle breeze and only ripples on the water, which was a dark brown colour.

The captain did not speak English, so it was up to Ahmed to point out the sights to them. After a while, he child left them alone to admire the scenery, including the boat traffic on the river.

The sun started to approach the western horizon, and the captain brought out a platter of cold delicacies, accompanied by a bottle of white wine. Sean and Amelia tried each in turn. They found themselves laughing a lot as they guessed at what was in each dish.

"The Nile here seems to be a relic of an earlier time, far away from the world that I'm familiar with," Amelia said. "It's as if we were visiting another planet, another age."

"I see what you mean. Even though we've all heard about Cairo and the Pharaohs, you really have to experience it in person to get a sense of what it's like."

The wine helped to make them mellow, and they started sharing details of their lives.

Back at the hotel, neither wanted the evening to end. After the Spartan atmosphere of Balabo, Egypt was a heady experience. It seemed natural to both of them when they ended up sharing Amelia's bed for the night.

The next morning they both were a little ashamed of themselves.

"You realize that this can't happen again," Amelia said, pulling up the covers around herself. "I don't know what got into me. If my father finds out, we'll both be in the doghouse!"

Sean nodded his head, but secretly hoped that their relationship could continue.

The next few days, while they waited to hear from Mukhtaar, they spent little time together. Instead, they wandered around Cairo and visited the museums on their own.

ARUSHA, OCTOBER 3-4

Mukhtaar was ensconced in the comfortable upholstered chair in the lobby of the airport hotel in Arusha, Tanzania. Facing him were Amelia and Sean, who had just flown in from Cairo. They were sitting at either end of a leather couch, with a space between them. Hassan noticed that they did not seem to be talking to each other.

Hassan was wearing a pair of slacks and a polo shirt, and he had a tall drink in his right hand. He seemed about ten years younger than the last time Sean had seen him.

Amelia questioned Hasson anxiously. "I was so relieved when we heard that you'd escaped from Summerland and were in Ethiopia! I thought it made sense to meet with you in Tanzania since my father said there's a job for you here if you want it. The manager of his mine left a few months ago, and he has been looking for a replacement. How did the trip go?"

"It was easier than I feared. I know some people in the westernmost province of Summerland, who live near to where your father's mine was located before the Summerland government closed it down. I took a bus from Balabo. They met me at the bus terminal, and drove me in an off-road vehicle along an old mining road across the border into Ethiopia where there are no customs posts. From there I took a bus to Addis, and then the Ethiopian Airlines flight to Arusha. I'll be happy to accept Mr. Armbrister's offer to become the manager of his mine here in Tanzania. I'm ready to start whenever he wants me to."

"My father plans to fly in tomorrow. I'm renting a Land Rover for him. He'll drive you to the mine and brief you on what needs to be done. In the meantime, can I pick your brain about the events in Summerland that have occurred since I lived there as a little girl? A lot has happened that I don't understand. What can you tell me about it?"

Mukhtaar took a sip at his drink, and leaned back in his chair. "This may take a while. You know that the country had become a dynamic and fast growing place, but also a place where there was great inequality. The elite, those who ran the government and who controlled the economy, were very wealthy, but the average person was still a peasant who grew a few subsistence crops, and if the family was lucky, owned an animal or two. People at the top, who had been educated abroad, were making a lot of money, but the common people didn't share in it. Building the casino was the last straw, because its patrons flaunted their wealth and impious behaviour. Mutterings of discontent became louder. Imams started decrying the activities of the infidels. The casino had become a centre for money laundering and prostitution."

"How was that allowed to happen?"

"The story I heard was that the casino owners bribed government ministers to give them a free hand. They even managed to get a consultants' report to support their position that the casino should be self-policing, and that gave cover for the ministers."

"So, what triggered the revolution?"

"The imams had indoctrinated many of the military, and this included some of the senior officers. When the election in 1998 gave no party a majority, threatening to throw the country into chaos, the army stepped in, declaring that the regime was suspended and a new Islamic constitution would be imposed. The generals were assigned key posts, as were senior members of the clergy.

"After the country stagnated for over a decade the junta realized that the country could not survive as an island cut off from the rest of the world, so they started to consider allowing foreign investment once again. Moreover, in 2018 the Chinese government made clear that their enterprises should not invest abroad in sex and gambling businesses, so that country was once again an acceptable partner for Summerland. China could build the roads, ports, and airports that the country needed. Summerland in turn was attractive to China because it was rich in minerals such as lithium, copper, and cobalt, needed by electric vehicles.

"So now we have some massive investments in infrastructure and mining, and the economy is on the move again. This time, there may be some trickle-down to the common citizen, since the projects require a lot of local labour. They also enrich our leaders, since Chinese companies are willing to pay bribes to get the approvals they need. There are rumours that some officials and government ministers have lavish private residences along the coast and money in Swiss banks. But the regime keeps a tight lid on the media and does not tolerate dissent, and so far, there is little public outcry."

Amelia nodded. "I knew all that, at least in general terms. But I need something more for my thesis. Is there some way to document the lead-up to the revolution, with details about the casino and why it ignited so much opposition in the country?"

"You can certainly find some newspaper reports about this episode, published in Summerland and elsewhere. But how you can get proof of the bribes paid by the casino owners I don't know."

"So, what happened to those who ran the casino, the hotel, and the marina for mega yachts? Did they leave the country, and if so, where could I find them?"

"You could try to locate the investors from Macau, but I doubt they would want to talk to you."

*****

Kevin Armbrister arrived on the KLM flight from Amsterdam, carrying only an overnight bag. He spotted the threesome at the arrivals gate and waved, before queuing for passport control. In a few minutes he was through, and he opened his arms wide to embrace Amelia.

"We've finally caught up to each other," he said happily. "Thank heavens you made it safely out of Summerland!" He nodded to Sean, and shook Mukhtaar's hand energetically. "So we meet again. It's good to see you, old friend! You know you can always find a job with my company, if you want one."

Turning back to his daughter, Kevin said: "I hope you'll come back to Canada with me. Enough gadding about the world! It's time to go home." He looked suspiciously at Sean. "I hope you two had a good time together in Balabo and Cairo. But now the party's over!"

Amelia scrunched her nose. "But I haven't found out what I wanted about the events in Summerland. I want to make a real contribution to our understanding of what happened."

Sean had been left out of the conversation, but now he interjected. "While Amelia goes back to Canada, I could go to Macau. I'll be happy to try to get the story of the casino from the Macanese investors, if you'll pay my expenses."

"We'll see about that," Armbrister replied gruffly.

OTTAWA, OCTOBER 5-6

Hamish contacted the three men who were the core group working on the casino in the 1990s. Roger Boudreau promised to get in touch with Hamish the next time he came to Ottawa for meetings at Global Affairs but did not volunteer any further information. John Kamara explained that he was not able to return to Canada any time soon, but would be happy to meet with him in Monrovia should the occasion arise. Clarence Chen was the only one who was still in North America, since he was temporarily living in Ottawa.

Hamish drove to the campus of Carleton University on the outskirts of Ottawa and managed to locate Clarence's office in the Loeb building. It was within sight of the Rideau River and the Rideau Canal. The weather was pleasant so they went outside and sat on a patio. Students were sunning themselves on the grass in front of them.

Chen seemed flustered by Hamish's visit. "Has anything new happened? Have you heard anything from Inspector Giroux?"

He was greying slightly at the temples, the only sign that he was no longer young. Hamish guessed that he must be about 60 now, but he didn't know for sure. He could pass for 40.

"I'd like to talk to you about the work on the casino in Balabo in the mid-1990s. I discovered that there was a project done for Summerland, despite the APTI board's refusal to get involved, and that you worked on it. Francis Chastain has admitted as much, and suggested that you and your colleagues didn't volunteer the information so as not to embarrass him."

Chen was grim faced. "Yes, that's so. Francis had agreed with the government to provide technical advice, despite the reluctance of the board. We all worked on the project because we thought we could help the country. At that stage they had decided to go ahead with the casino anyway, and we felt they needed our advice to make the project work and minimize its unfavourable effects. Tragically, our efforts came to nought. I didn't want Francis's long period of public service to be stained by that failure."

"So you worked with Roger Boudreau and John Kamara, going to Balabo and consulting with government officials?"

"Most of the work was done in Ottawa. We put together an outline of the measures we thought the Summerlanders needed to enact to regulate the casino, drawing on the experience of other jurisdictions. Then we went to Balabo–the three of us, plus Francis Chastain and the desk officer Terence Deaver–to make a presentation there. That was the extent of our work."

"So Francis did go to Balabo? He claims he's never been there."

"Yes he did go, and even stayed there for a few days after the rest of us departed. He explained that he knew one of the backers of the casino, who had invited him to stay on his yacht."

Hamish sat up angrily. "You do realize that taking gifts or bonuses from governments or private individuals was explicitly forbidden at APTI?"

"Francis explained that this was a grey area, and that the Summerlanders would be insulted if we didn't accept their generosity. What's the saying: 'When in Rome, do as the Romans'?"

"So what did you get out of it, aside from a generous salary?"

"Nothing really, just a souvenir or two."

Hamish snarled: "For example, a valuable pearl?"

Chen looked abashed. "I guess. I gave it to my girlfriend at the time. I don't see her anymore and I don't know what became of it."

"Well, Francis gave Adele a very handsome pearl, and she's still wearing it. I bet he received other 'souvenirs' too! What can you tell me about that friend of Chastain's who invited him onto his yacht?"

"Nothing much; I never met him. Francis said that they'd been roommates at Oxford. I think he's an Englishman, but lives in Macau." He sighed. "I hope you aren't going to hound Francis, he's done a lot of good over his career. I admit that Summerland was a mistake, but how was he to know?"

"The issue is whether his judgement may have been clouded by the inducements that he received from the backers of the casino. Maybe bad things might have happened anyway, but that's not an excuse for ignoring bribery and corruption!" Hamish, who was usually calm, found himself unable to suppress his anger.

Chen recoiled, and shook his head. "That's going too far! Francis would never do that!"

"Let me ask you something else, related to the party and Bob Wismer's death. You said you heard the sound of an engine before the storm that occurred around 2 a.m. What sort of engine was it–a car, a truck, or perhaps a boat? Did you hear any talking? Could Bob have gone outside to meet someone?"

"I'd say a car or a truck, though I'm not sure. I was groggy from my sleeping pills. I didn't hear any voices, but if people were talking outside their words might have been too faint."

*****

The next morning Hamish was in Tim Blacket's office, indignantly recounting his conversation with Clarence Chen. "In spite of all the respect I have for the Francis Chastain I used to work for, what he did in Summerland can't just be swept under the carpet. I think you should ask the board of APTI to reprimand him and the others for taking gifts in contravention of their employment contracts. You can't turn a blind eye to this."

Blacket shifted in his chair uneasily. "I'm not sure that a reprimand would serve any useful purpose, except to besmirch the organization. After all, Francis is retired now."

"Well, if I write the history of APTI then it will come out in the open, and the Institute will be forced to do something about it."

"So you've decided to take the commission? I should warn you that before we publish it, we will read it carefully and may require editorial changes."

Hamish glared at him. "Then I don't want to write it. Find someone else. Maybe Francis himself will do it, now that suspicions are starting to swirl around him. It would give him a chance to whitewash his activities." He laughed maliciously.

"Listen, Hamish, I'll hire you to follow up with your inquiries of Chastain's behaviour relative to Summerland on a confidential basis, and I'll present your findings to the board. They will decide whether to sanction him. But whatever they decide, it won't be made public. Can you agree to that?"

Hamish gave it a moment's thought, then nodded. "I'll charge the usual rate for my time and expect APTI to cover my travel expenses. And be aware that I will go to the police with any findings that point to criminal behaviour."

They shook hands on it.

MACAU, OCTOBER 6-7

Sean flew Emirates Airlines to Macau via Dubai. Armbrister had agreed to pay for the trip, more as a present for Amelia than because he was optimistic that Sean would discover anything of interest. He did have the name of someone who had been involved in running the casino in Balabo. Richard Owens was currently listed as the manager of one of the Macanese casinos. Sean hoped he could get in to see him if he was on the spot. Trying to get an appointment beforehand seemed counterproductive.

In the taxi from the airport Sean was awed by the tall casino buildings and their garish decorations. He had heard that there were more than 40 of them now. He gaped at the Venetian, named after the Las Vegas casino but considerably larger, comprising a shopping mall, a 3,000 room hotel, and, of course, canals with gondoliers. Sean had a reservation at a more modest hotel in Taipa associated with one of the older casinos, where Owens was the manager. The casino dated back to the time, before Macau was returned to China by Portugal in 1999, when Stanley Ho controlled all the casinos in the territory. The big Las Vegas casinos–the Venetian, Sands, MGM Grand, and Wynn–were only given permission to operate in Macau in the early years of the 21st century after the mainland Chinese took control. The foreign casinos were now a major presence.

The hotel lobby was glitzy, with shiny black marble counters and stylish stainless steel tables and chairs. His room, though small, had all the amenities he expected, including a minibar and a Jacuzzi. After changing his clothes, Sean wandered down to the least formal of the hotel's restaurants, a noodle bar, and ate a bowl of wonton noodles with shrimp, washed down with a beer. *Delicious. I think I'm going to like it here!*

The next day Sean visited the casino itself. It was in one of the smaller buildings, and less extravagantly decorated than the big casinos. He entered through the revolving doors, and walked up to the reception desk. A Chinese man in a dark grey Mao jacket and matching slacks greeted him.

Sean put on a polite smile. "I'd like to speak to the manager, please. Mr. Richard Owens."

"Is it something I can help you with? Why do you want to see him?"

"It's a private matter, I would like to talk to him personally."

The man looked sceptical. "I'm afraid you will need to make an appointment. Please call his secretary." He gave Sean a card that listed the casino's phone numbers.

Sean took out one of his business cards, as well as the Ocean Pearl gaming chip that he had picked up in Balabo. "Would you give him my card and this chip? I think he will want to talk to me."

The man looked at both sides of the gambling chip, a puzzled expression on his face. "I'll see if he's available." He walked from the reception desk to the rear of the lobby, pushed a button beside a door, and was buzzed through. After a minute, he re-emerged, and motioned for Sean to approach.

"Mr. Owens will see you now." He held the door for Sean to enter, closed it with a click indicating that it was once again locked, and led him to one of the offices along a corridor.

The room was sparsely furnished, with just a desk and a swivel chair behind it, and a nondescript couch. A bank of file cabinets occupied one side of the room. A few framed photos adorned the walls.

The man behind the desk got up to greet Sean. He stuck out his hand. "I'm Richard Owens, and I gather you're a private detective who wants to talk about Summerland's Ocean Pearl casino. Normally I don't agree to see walk-ins without an appointment, but I'm intrigued. What can I do for you?"

Sean was encouraged by Owens' British civility. "Nice to meet you, and thanks for seeing me. I've just been to Balabo, and I'm trying to understand what happened to make the country close down the casino and shut itself off from the outside world. Was there a particular incident that triggered this? I gather you were the manager there. Oh, and do you mind if I record our conversation?"

"Fine, you can record it, but be aware that I'm not going to reveal any confidential details about the casino in Balabo that I managed. At the time our organization ran all the casinos here in Macau, and we were keen to expand outside the territory. We supplied some of the capital to build the casino in Balabo, and the rest came from other Macanese investors. We managed the project. Once we got the approval from the Summerland government we brought in the construction materials from mainland China, and Chinese labour did most of the work."

"So you went there once it was built, to run the casino itself?"

"Correct. It went smoothly at first. The Summerland government was a big supporter of the casino. It saw how much money we made here in Macau, and that everybody gained. That's why the average income here is so high. Of course, there are some very rich people and some who only make enough to scrape by, but there are jobs for everyone. Moreover, the Macau government keeps taxes low because of the income it gets from the casinos."

"So what happened in Summerland to change people's minds?"

"Officials there were too greedy. Everyone wanted a slice of the pie, whether they did any work for the casino or not. Of course we had to buy off the government ministers involved in the project, but it extended down through the bureaucracy. The backers of the casino did not properly do their research into its profitability. They didn't factor in the fact that a casino in Africa is a very different proposition from those in Macau or Las Vegas. In Macau we have millions of well-heeled gamblers who live nearby, some of whom come to the territory from Hong Kong just for the day. Balabo was a very different story. All the business at the casino was with foreigners who came from a long way off, some from South Africa, but most from Europe or Asia. We couldn't generate the profits of the casinos here because Ocean Pearl had nowhere near the gambling volume. So we decided we had to aim for the high-end market, and attract the ultra-wealthy by providing a place to dock their yachts, an exotic but safe destination for them to visit."

"That wasn't in the plan from the beginning?"

"No, the idea came from our main private investor, Sir Harold Feenstra, who lives here in Macau but is often embarked on his motor yacht, Xanadu, sailing around the Indian Ocean or the Mediterranean. He was the one who came up with the marina plans, and financed its construction. He also suggested to us that we build a luxury hotel next to the casino, which we constructed jointly with him."

"This was a few years later then? And did this help boost profitability?"

"Unfortunately not. The number of people whose palms we had to grease increased commensurately. While Sir Harold benefitted from having a place to keep his yacht, there was little other business. The hotel was a big money loser, since it was never filled to capacity. So we were thinking of winding down the casino when the Islamic revolution came. In a way it was a godsend, since we were able to get some compensation from our insurance policies. Macau underwent a tremendous expansion in the early years of this century, so no longer being involved abroad was a good thing for us!"

"Interesting ... But what triggered the revolution, to your mind?"

Owens hesitated, visibly bothered by the question. "Opinions differ, but one thing is certain: the checks on illegal activities associated with the casino were absent in Summerland. We tried to weed out the customers who seemed to be laundering dirty money, but it wasn't really our job. We're not into law enforcement; that's up to the authorities. But the gambling commission in Summerland never did anything. So there were a lot of shady things going on, such as people bringing suitcases of money to buy gambling chips. The Summerland government didn't care. The ministers were making money hand over fist."

"I understand that a Canadian institute advised the government on how to manage gambling in the country. Didn't they recommend strict oversight?"

"That's what's strange. They did recommend it in a meeting with government officials, but then they didn't follow up on their recommendations so they implicitly approved the government's inaction. By the second half of the decade Balabo had become a sort of den of iniquity, attracting all sorts of criminal activities. It was so flagrant that the clergy could not ignore it, and imams started to rail against the infidels. When the 1998 election was inconclusive and the country seemed to be veering toward chaos, the army stepped in, with the support of the mosques."

"I gather that the military junta is opening up the country once again to Chinese investment."

"That's true, from what I read in the papers. But this has no connection with the earlier period. After all, Macau was not attached to China then. And, in 2018, Xi Jinping issued a directive that Chinese companies should not invest abroad in ventures involving gambling or sex. We have no intention of trying to re-establish a casino on the African continent."

"I see. Well, Richard, if I may call you by your first name, you've been very helpful. Thank you for your time."

"It's been a pleasure to relive old times. Despite everything, I have many happy memories of my stint in Balabo." Owens shook Sean's hand and escorted him out to the lobby.

"Oh, and I forgot. Here's your Ocean Pearl gambling chip back."

*****

Sean considered that he had got the information he had come for, though Amelia might be disappointed. Summerland in the 1990s had not been a battleground among the great powers, and the revolution did not result from any machinations among them. Instead, events seemed to have been driven by greed–on the part of the casino backers and of Summerland officials. He hoped that Amelia nevertheless would have enough material to write her thesis. He checked that his cell phone had indeed recorded the conversation with Richard Owens and uploaded it to Google Drive.

Before flying out the next day, Sean decided to see some of the local sights. He took the ferry to Hong Kong, staying on deck as the boat made the brief crossing of the Zhujiang River estuary. He marvelled at the stunning views of steep mountains and mysterious islands covered in lush vegetation. After presenting his passport and clearing customs, he wandered around the crowded streets, looking at the street markets and stores selling all sorts of foods and handicrafts, as well as electronics and household appliances.

He started to feel claustrophobic as the sea of humanity swept around him. *I'd better not stray too far from the ferry dock.* He stepped into a bar to get away from the crowds, and ordered a Black Kite pale ale. The bar was mostly empty in mid-afternoon, and Sean's heart rate settled back to normal in the relative calm after the frenzy outside.

After half an hour he headed back to the ferry for the return trip. As he left the bar, a heavy-set man wearing a traditional cheongsam bumped into him, knocking him off balance. He managed to retain his footing by grabbing a lamppost with both hands. The man did not apologize but kept going, and was soon swallowed up by the crowd.

Sean felt in his pockets. His passport was still there, but his wallet was missing, as was his smartphone. *Damn! It's a good thing that I left most of my cash and my credit cards in my room safe. This will teach me to get a money belt next time!*

The next day Sean took a non-stop Cathay Pacific flight from Hong Kong to Toronto, and an Air Canada flight to Halifax. He emerged from the terminal into mild fall weather and joined the queue for a taxi. *A long trip, but less arduous than the flight to Balabo. It's good to be back in a temperate climate! I'm looking forward to seeing Amelia again also.*

GATINEAU AND OTTAWA, OCTOBER 7-9

The Gatineau Police headquarters on Boulevard Gréber was nearly deserted on this Friday evening. Inspecteur Giroux listlessly leafed through the documents he had on the death of Robert Wismer and the fire at his cottage. None of it made any sense to him.

Why would a man get up around 2 a.m. to go down slippery stone steps to his dock in the dark? Maybe he had an open boat down there that he was afraid would sink from all the rain? But there was no boat when I arrived to look at the body floating in the river, and no one mentioned one ever being there.

All the evidence suggests that Vismère slipped and hit his head on a rock—the rock that was found near the water. That should have wrapped up the case, and I wouldn't have to worry about what Vismère was doing. But then why was the cottage torched the next day? That wasn't an accident. The fire marshal made it clear that it could only be arson.

The two events a day apart can't just be a coincidence. But what is the connection? Does that mean that Vismère's death was murder, or did someone just take advantage of the cottage being empty to set fire to it? But if so, why? None of this makes any sense.

And now the boss is putting pressure on me to show some progress. The RCMP takes an interest in the safety of senior government officials, and especially international civil servants, and now they are starting to say unkind things about the Gatineau police. The boss wants this case closed. But what could I do that I've not already done? If only I had grilled those guys who were at the party for that bigwig Chastain. At least he has a French name, even though it appears that he doesn't speak a word. What about that other guy, that smart ass from Nova Scotia, the private detective? I think I'll just give him a call, and threaten him a little, see what turns up.

He dialled the cell number on the card that Hamish had given him.

"Hello, Cameron here."

"This is Inspecteur Giroux. We are still investigating Monsieur Vismère's death, and we would like you to give us a detailed timetable of what you were doing while staying at his cottage."

"Am I a suspect?"

"As you can well understand, everyone who was staying at the cottage is a potential suspect. And you were the one who found his body, as well as the only person who was still there when the cottage was set on fire. So can I have a list of your activities for those two days?"

Hamish growled: "I've already done that, both when you came to examine the body and after the fire. I have nothing further to add."

Giroux grumbled to himself, but he could think of no rejoinder, so he swallowed his pride. "Okay, Okay, I get your point. Help me out here; we're at a dead end. What do you think happened? What's the connection between the fire and Vismère's death?"

Hamish lost his patience. "I already told you: I think that the link between the two is the fact that Bob Wismer brought up the work of the APTI on a casino in Summerland, in the 1990s. I'm convinced that the guest list at Chastain's party was chosen among those who had worked on the casino project, and Chastain himself was involved with that East African country. He's admitted that to me since, though he denied it at the party. There has to be someone who felt threatened by Bob's probing for a book on the history of APTI that he was hired to write by its president."

"I don't know anything about all that. I'm out of my depth here. So you think it was murder after all? We have no evidence to prove it. There's only one set of footprints leading down to the water, and that's yours."

"I'm not sure. But if I were you, I'd look into Bob Wismer's activities in the few weeks before his death. Maybe he talked to someone about this, and it could be that others were aware that he had incriminating evidence that was kept at the cottage. And you could sift through the debris at the cottage to see if there are any clues about why the place was torched, though it's probably too late for that."

"All right, I'll talk to the executor, the lawyer guy. I've got to show my boss that I'm doing something." His tone had changed from blustering to grovelling. He pleaded. "Keep me informed if you learn something more about this."

*****

Jessica was as perfectly coiffed and elegantly dressed as ever. Hamish met her at a new Ottawa restaurant on Bank Street that boasted fresh seafood "right off the boat." Hamish remarked to her that it was more likely that the fish was freshly frozen on the boat, then shipped by air to Ottawa from Halifax. "But the menu looks good, and I think I will try the bouillabaisse. What about you?"

"The glazed salmon with au gratin potatoes and wilted greens. So what have you been up to, Hamish?"

"Tim has actually hired me to look into the activities of APTI in Summerland. I think he did this because he didn't want me to go public with accusations against anyone at APTI who might have been involved in improprieties. I'm to give him a report which he'll share with the board; they'll decide what to do about it. So they can hush it up if they like, whether or not they sanction any current or past employees. But I've made it clear that if I discover anything criminal I'll have to report it to the police."

"Have you made any progress? What do you suspect?"

"I've had some more conversations with Francis Chastain, who now admits that he was more heavily involved in the work on Summerland than he let on before. Clarence Chen also claims that Francis went to Balabo with a team composed of Chen,

Boudreau, and Kamara, to present their recommendations on the legal and economic regulations that should accompany the opening of a casino. This work was financed by the Chinese government, out of APTI's special funds. Apparently, they received a bonus over and above their salaries, and each was given gifts–at least a valuable pearl, and perhaps other things."

"Then your report can clearly highlight that APTI's regulations were broken, whether or not the institute can do anything about it, now that all those concerned are no longer employed. So are you finished your work for them?"

"I think there must be more to learn. I don't understand why Francis would have done this, and in the process endanger his reputation, risk being sanctioned by APTI, and perhaps lose his job."

"Francis was besotted with Adele at the time, and he had just gone through a messy divorce. Perhaps he needed the money? He certainly gave her a lot of presents, including a gold necklace with a very large pearl. Adele was captivated by it, and showed it off to the women in the office."

"She still wears it. I saw it around her neck when I went to speak to Francis. I think it came from Summerland. Incidentally, where is their house in Ottawa? I've only visited them in Gatineau, in their cottage along the river."

"They have a very handsome house in Rockcliffe, which Francis bought shortly after their marriage. So I guess at that point he was flush with money, because as you know, Rockcliffe Park is the most expensive neighbourhood in Ottawa. It's still the place to live, and the home of many bigwigs."

They dug into their food when it was brought to the table, and did not discuss APTI again. After passing up dessert, they both settled their bills by credit card.

"This has been a very pleasant dinner, and it's good to see you again," Hamish said with a smile. "But I also have a favour to ask. Would you mind looking at the files on Summerland that I retrieved from Bob's house and those that Terence Deaver's widow gave me? I had them in the trunk of my car, so they didn't get destroyed in the fire. I've examined them myself, but I'm not very familiar with the material. I didn't know Bob well or Terence at all. Perhaps you can find something that I missed."

"Sure, Hamish, I can do that. If you've got them with you, just put them in my car."

*****

Jessica called Hamish the next day. "I have a few ideas that came to me while reading the files. It might be best to sit down and look through them together, and I'll explain. How about meeting for lunch at Benny's Bistro in the Byward Market? I love their food, especially their pastries. Let's eat late, after the office crowd clears out."

The cafe was still fairly crowded when they arrived a little before two, but they did manage to get a table that was large enough to spread out the two sets of files.

"Here's what I found that pricked my curiosity," Jessica explained. "There's the budget allocation to the project, which Bob mentioned at the party. You've figured out that it was financed by the Chinese, through the country funds. But there's also a note in Deaver's files saying that they should contact Harold Feenstra for details about the plans for the casino. I looked him up, and he was one of the investors from Macau. I wonder if Terence's agenda, which has a number of entries saying 'meet with F' might refer to Feenstra, not Francis. What do you think?"

"Possibly. Clarence Chen said that Francis stayed on the yacht of one of the backers of the project in Balabo, someone he knew from his student days at Oxford. I'll check Feenstra out, to see if there's a connection there. Anything else?"

"It's curious that there is no copy in either set of files of the report of the team on the measures needed to regulate, tax, and police the casino. This was presumably the whole object of the exercise, why APTI got involved, and what China paid for, either because they wanted to help out Summerland or use it for their own purposes when they took over Macau. But where is the report? Maybe for reasons of confidentiality the only copies printed were given to the Chinese and Summerland governments, but you would think that there would be at least a draft in one of the files. I wonder why there isn't."

"Interesting. I'll try to get more info out of Clarence Chen. He must remember what was in the report and to whom it was given."

"One last thing. Since Bob and I were both working downtown I kept up with him, and we occasionally did lunch. He told me that he had agreed to take on writing the history of APTI, and that he thought the book would be explosive. So I think he knew more than he let on about at the party. He may have been goading Francis. I'll bet the reason for the party was not to mark his retirement but rather to focus attention on his activities in Summerland. Francis or one of the others might well have felt threatened by this."

"What else might he have known? And why is there no record of it in Bob's files?"

"That's a puzzle. As you said the other day at dinner, there's more here that needs to be investigated."

"I've talked again to the Gatineau policeman, Giroux, and I tried to convince him that the reason for Bob's death and the fire might be what happened in Summerland in the 1990s. But he doesn't take me seriously. I wonder if you would do something for me–talk to Adele. I don't think I could find an excuse to get her alone, but as an old friend maybe you could. Would you do that?"

"Hmm, I'm not sure, but I could try. We did both hang out with a group of other women at APTI in the day, but that was a long time ago. I haven't seen her for years, except for the odd formal reception when she accompanies Francis. I'll see what I can do. Perhaps a celebration for a mutual friend … but what do you hope to get from her?"

"I don't know. Just talk to her about what happened, and get her suspicions or insights."

They left it there. Hamish walked Jessica to her car. She turned, and this time gave him a peck on his cheek. "Hamish, it was good to meet with you again. I almost hope this investigation goes on for a long time, so I can see more of you!" She laughed, and said, "Arrivederci."

HALIFAX, OCTOBER 9

Back in Canada, Sean met with Kevin Armbrister and Amelia at Truro Resources' offices. Sean and Amelia pretended to be only acquaintances, but when her father wasn't looking she gave him a smile. Hamish had just flown in from Ottawa, and he joined them a few minutes later as well. The weather had finally turned cold, and everyone was glad to be indoors and out of the elements.

"I did get a good interview with Richard Owens, who was happy to talk about the Ocean Pearl casino," Sean said. "I recorded the conversation on my phone, and fortunately I then uploaded the recording to the cloud, because my phone got stolen in Hong Kong. We can listen to it if you like." Turning to Amelia, he added: "I think you'll find this useful for your thesis."

Armbrister nodded. "Sure, let's do that. I'll get my secretary to bring in tea and coffee in the meantime."

After the recording had ended, Hamish commented: "The puzzle is still why the casino was not kept under strict control by the government. After all, the APTI project was financed by the Chinese explicitly to work out the regulatory environment. We don't have their report, but we can only assume it treated in some detail the anti-money-laundering regulations and other enforcement issues. They seem to have been totally ignored."

"I have another question," Amelia said. "Why did the Chinese finance the study? Don't forget Macau didn't become a Chinese territory until 1999, so they were not directly concerned by the casino. Perhaps they wanted to use the study for their own purposes, and apply its recommendations to Macau when they took over? Or maybe they wanted to make sure that the investment in Summerland by Macau didn't throw discredit onto Chinese investments generally."

"There's another mystery," Sean added. "Whose decision was it to shelve the report, and why did they do so? It was in the interest of the casino owners not to be under the thumb of the government, but Owens admitted that he was surprised that there was so little oversight."

Armbrister got up to pour himself another cup of tea. "Sir Harold Feenstra was heavily involved in the casino, the marina, and the hotel. He would know the answers to the questions, but will he tell us? I met him when we were living in Balabo. The construction of the casino was just getting underway, and he was spending much of his time in Summerland. I'm sure he remembers me. We had a number of pleasant evenings together at the Hotel Metropole—which sadly closed many years ago."

Hamish nodded. "It's worth a try. I'd also be curious to know whether he's Francis Chastain's buddy from Oxford. Chastain is the person who seems to have arranged for APTI to prepare the report for Summerland on behalf of the Chinese."

"Fine, then, I'll try to contact him."

Hamish put on the table the photo that Jessica Bowles had given him. He pointed out Francis Chastain to Armbrister.

Sean leaned over to have a look. "Wait a minute, I think I recognize that fellow!" pointing to Clarence Chen. "That's the guy I saw at the hotel in Balabo and at the Mining Commission!"

"That's impossible! He said he was going to a conference in Toronto when I saw him at Bob Wismer's cottage."

"Well, maybe he flew to Balabo afterward," Sean replied.

OTTAWA, OCTOBER 11-13

Jessica Bowles gave Adele Chastain a call and she answered at the second ring. "Adele, I'm calling to invite you to a going-away party for Susie Follows. Do you remember her from APTI? She's been working here at Global Affairs, and she's going to retire and move out to BC this winter. The party will be at the Chateau Laurier this Friday."

Adele took a moment to react to the unexpected call, then said: "So nice to hear from you, Jessica, after all this time! Yes, of course I remember Susie, and I'd love to come. It will be nice to catch up with her and some other people I knew at APTI. I've lost touch with most of them. My life has become so boring."

Two days later, Adele was one of the first to arrive at the Chateau Laurier, having been lucky in finding a parking space right away between the hotel and the National Gallery. Jessica was there to greet her at the door of the meeting room where the party was being held. Adele was wearing a designer pants suit, light blue, and brown pumps made by Gucci. Around her neck was her gold necklace with the single large pearl.

Jessica admired her appearance. "You look lovely, Adele. I remember that necklace. You showed it to us girls about the time you got engaged to Francis. Where did he get it? I've never seen anything like it! "

"Yes, it's my favourite. I believe he had the necklace made here, to showcase a pearl that he brought back from Summerland. He's given me nothing half as nice since then!"

Jessica laughed. "You don't do too badly in the clothing line, it seems to me! But tell me, what do you do with yourself? Do you miss working?"

"Not the work, just the friends and colleagues. I get lonely at the cottage, where we spend much of the summer. It's pretty isolated. I do a lot of swimming, and some boating. It keeps me fit."

"You certainly seem very trim." Jessica looked at her slyly. "Did you ever see much of Bob Wismer? I remember your cottage and his are not too far apart."

Adele's face fell. "What a tragedy. Yes, he was a friend. I won't say anything more than that."

"Anyway, come on in and meet Susie and the others. And the bar is over there if you want to have something to drink."

*****

Giroux contacted the lawyer who was executor for Bob Wismer's estate, and who had also been Bob's friend. Tony Francesca had his own legal practice, mainly doing real estate and wills. He agreed to come to the Gatineau Police station to be interviewed.

Giroux invited the lawyer to sit in a chair on the other side of his desk. "Merci d'être venu. You've now had about a month to examine Monsieur Vismère's affairs, and I hope you can tell us what you've learned about his recent activities and the state of his finances. We're still looking for clues about his death and the fire the next day at his cottage. Have you come across anything that sheds light on them?"

Francesca scratched his chin. "What do you have in mind? I've been through the usual financial information, contacted his bank, gotten his will out of a safety deposit box, put an obituary in the newspapers, and notified next of kin, in addition to arranging for his funeral."

"Any large or repeated payments into or out of his bank account, aside from utility bills or taxes?"

"No, nothing like that."

"Who benefits from his death?"

"Aside from a few charities and small legacies to friends and distant relatives, Bob's estate will go to his son, his only offspring."

"Aha! So his son had a motive. And have you contacted him?"

"Yes, I managed to notify him of his father's death by phone. He's been in Thailand for the past few months. I'm quite sure that he was out of the country at the time of Bob's demise."

"Oh. Well then, did you find anything unusual in his papers? Did he keep a diary?"

"His records seem to have gone up in smoke, and his diary too, if he kept one."

"How familiar are you with his personal life? Did he have enemies? A romantic interest? Has he ever been threatened, or felt threatened?"

"I think you're touching on things that could be protected by attorney-client confidentiality. I will say though that he recently told me he was in love, had picked up with an old flame, and they were thinking of living together. But you should realize that Bob was a bit of a womanizer, and it's not the first time he's said that. He didn't mention her name, and I didn't ask. Now, is that all?"

"Be sure to keep me informed should you acquire further information. You can go now."

HALIFAX AND NASSAU, OCTOBER 15-20

Armbrister was downcast when he contacted Sean. "I called my friend Harold Feenstra's office in Macau but was told that he was not available. Apparently, he's on his yacht somewhere–the Xanadu. Since they wouldn't give me his sat phone number there's no way to reach him. I could ask his office to relay a message but I don't want to do that. I just want to chat with him."

"You know, we can find where he is because the Automatic Identification System tracks the location of ships everywhere on the globe. Every vessel of a certain size has to have an AIS communication device that reports its location. This helps prevent collisions at sea. It also allows importers, for instance, to know where their shipment is so they can estimate its arrival time. Feenstra's yacht is certainly big enough to require it. Let me get onto a tracking app to see where he is."

After a few moments with his laptop, Sean said: "Hmm, it looks as though he must be on this side of the Atlantic, among the islands of the Bahamas."

"Great! See if you can find out more precisely where the Xanadu is located. I was thinking of taking a vacation down there. I could arrange to be around when he gets off his boat, in Nassau or wherever."

Sean smiled. "Can I come too?"

"Sure, I could use the company."

*****

On the flight down to Nassau's Lynden Pindling airport Amelia reminded her father why she had to be on the trip: "I started this whole inquiry into Summerland. I need to be the one speaking to Feenstra. I'm the one writing the thesis."

"And I'm the one paying for it," Armbrister said wryly. "Oh well, I guess I should continue to humour you."

Sean handed the guide book to Nassau back to Kevin. "He's docked at the Marina at Atlantis, which can accommodate a number of superyachts. It's not going to be easy to get close to his ship, however. Security there is supposed to be pretty tight."

"That's going to be your job, Sean. I'm guessing that he will be doing some sightseeing, so we should be able to bump into him somewhere if you tell us where he is."

"How will I recognize him?"

"I've got some photos of him, though they're decades old. So I searched online and I found that he has appeared several times recently in the society pages of the South China Morning Post, with pictures. I've made copies." He handed them to Sean and Amelia.

The WestJet flight passed low over the mansions and boat slips of Lyford Cay before smoothly landing at Nassau airport. After a long walk to the passport control counters and a short wait for luggage, they took a cab to Paradise Island and checked into the Royal, the largest of the Atlantis hotels.

*****

The Xanadu was visible from the entrance to the marina, as it towered over neighbouring boats. The ship had three decks, and a helipad on its top deck. There was no one visible aboard. Sean looked around for a good vantage point to keep a watch on the gangplank of the ship. Access to the dock itself required a magnetic card. He settled on a bar that gave a view out over the marina. Since it was 11 o'clock Sean reckoned that the sun was over the yardarm, so he ordered a Kalik beer and settled in to read the Nassau Guardian.

An hour later a man in a white naval uniform stepped off the ship and walked past the window where Sean was sitting. Sean stayed at his place, but had a good look at the other man's face so that he would recognize him again. After another half hour, he was getting really bored, having finished reading the paper and doing all its puzzles.

Just as he was considering giving up, a large man clad in grey slacks and a blue blazer came down the gangway, followed by a blond-haired woman easily 40 years his junior. She was wearing blue jeans and a tight short-sleeved pink blouse that showed off the curves of her bosom. Wrap-around sunglasses masked her face.

Sean checked the photo that Armbrister had given him, and concluded that it must be Harold Feenstra. He got up and sauntered out the door a few seconds after the pair had passed in front of the window. Keeping well behind them, he followed as they walked along the paths within Atlantis, passing the Royal and stopping at the Cove Pool, a place for outdoor gaming. Feenstra settled at the games table, motioning over a waiter and ordering something to drink for himself and his companion. After taking a sip from his glass, he joined a blackjack game at the moment the dealer opened a new deck of cards.

Sean, who was observing them from a distance, pulled out his cell phone and called Armbrister. "He's at the Cove Pool, and it looks as though he might be here for a while."

Half an hour later, Kevin and Amelia entered Cove Pool. They sat at a table on the patio away from the gaming tables. Feenstra was still playing blackjack, and had a large stack of chips in front of him. He was concentrating on the cards when they were turned over, both the dealer's and those of the two other players, and did not notice them arrive. After another two hands, he slid a couple of red chips over to the dealer, gathered up his remaining chips, and stood up, as did his companion. They started over to the nearby outdoor restaurant.

Armbrister quickly got up, motioning Amelia to stay where she was, and walked in their direction. He waved and said in a loud voice, "Sir Harold! It's good to see you again."

Feenstra stopped, puzzled. "Do I know you?"

"It's Kevin Armbrister. We knew each other in Summerland. It's been a long time though."

"Oh, right. How are you Kevin?" He stuck out his hand. "I've just been amusing myself with a little blackjack. Why don't you join us for a light meal? We're going to the fish restaurant over there."

"Sure, I'd love to. Let me introduce you to my daughter." He motioned to Amelia, who got up to join them.

The waiter took their orders, Feenstra and his companion, whom he introduced as Shirley, chose cracked conch, while Armbrister ordered a spiny lobster tail and Amelia a grouper fillet. Feenstra decided on a bottle of sparkling white wine, which the waiter poured out into four glasses.

Sir Harold mentioned that they were staying on his yacht, and that he was here partially on business. "I'm scouting around the Bahamas for a good place to build a casino, and enjoying visiting the various islands while I do so. I also like to do a little gambling, especially playing blackjack. That was how I got into the casino business in the first place. I have a photographic memory, so I can usually keep track of all the cards that have been played. I earned a First in maths at Oxford, so I recalculate the odds of getting a winning hand as the dealer goes through the deck. Normally the casino can spot gamblers who count cards at blackjack, and they kick them out, but they know me and so they let me do it." He laughed.

Shirley burbled. "He usually wins enough to buy me some nice clothes, and Nassau is a great place to shop!"

"Amelia and I are here on a short holiday. She just visited Balabo again, to relive some of the experiences there when she was just a young girl. But it's certainly changed, hasn't it, Amelia?"

"Not for the better, either! I felt I was being watched all the time. I don't know what happened to make a tropical paradise into a concentration camp!"

Feenstra chuckled. "Yes, that's a good description. I haven't been back since they closed down my casino and made it clear that I wasn't welcome any more."

"So, what was it like running a casino there?"

"It was a mistake. The company I partnered with didn't do a proper job researching the market. We had hoped to attract a lot of well-heeled gamblers from South Africa and Saudi Arabia, as well as Europe and Asia, but that didn't happen. And the marina I built should have been a haven for the mega yacht crowd, but piracy in the Red Sea made many of them leery of coming. Government oversight threatened to further increase our costs by keeping people away, so we bought off some of the ministers and the consultants who recommended beefing up taxation and law enforcement. But then everything fell apart. We never got the government to give us any compensation when the military junta closed us down. Fortunately we had insurance."

"What was it that triggered the military takeover?" Amelia interjected.

"There was an incident at the casino. Normally we allowed workers to reduce their hours of work during Ramadan, to accommodate fasting during the day and eating at night. But that year, we unexpectedly got an influx of business so we forced our croupiers and restaurant staff to work long hours. The Muslim clerics seized on this as an assault against the Islamic religion, and they whipped up opposition to the regime. When the election took place, the result of voting was a standoff between the religious based candidates and the party in power. The army took the side of the former, and ousted the existing government, putting their leaders in jail. We had only a few days to close up shop and get out of the country."

"Tell me about this consultants' report, and how you managed to get them to back off." Armbrister said with a laugh, as if making a joke.

"They recommended a strict regime that would have forced us to vet all our customers and to ban undesirables who might be involved in organized crime in their own countries. That would have made our business impossible to run. Moreover, they demanded that there be a police presence at the casino, and strict enforcement of a ban on prostitution. That was a non-starter for us. In Macau, we are given a free hand by the Chinese government as long as we don't let things become a threat to public order. Fortunately, the consultant in Balabo was someone I knew from uni and he toned down his report. For a price." Feenstra chuckled.

"But all that is history. Now I'm focussed on expanding in the Bahamas and elsewhere on this side of the Atlantic. The Bahamas is pretty well served with casinos, however, both here in Nassau and on Grand Bahama. I'm going next to Abaco to see if now would be a good time to establish one there, while they're still rebuilding from Hurricane Dorian."

Shirley, who seemed to be daydreaming, sat up. "I hear that they have one of the greatest beaches there at Treasure Cay. I'll get a chance to work on my tan! I hope there's shopping there too."

"Sorry darling, I don't think there's much for you to buy there. You'll have to walk to Bay Street this afternoon to get your shopping fix." He looked at her lasciviously. "Then we can have some fun in Xanadu's pool."

*****

Since neither Kevin nor Amelia was a gambler, they wandered off when Feenstra resumed his blackjack after lunch. Sean had abandoned his post and had gotten a snack at one of the poolside bars. He rejoined them as they walked back to the hotel.

Armbrister was keen to do some snorkelling, and the three of them settled on a catamaran cruise that departed from the Paradise Island ferry terminal, a short walk from the hotel. Amelia changed into a bikini and wore a t-shirt and cut-offs over it.

The sun was warm and the water a beautiful turquoise as they cast off from the dock. The crew raised the sails and they ghosted in silence toward a reef off the north side of New Providence Island. Amelia excitedly pointed out two dolphins accompanying them, playfully diving in and out of the boat's bow wave. Once they had anchored, guests were issued with masks and flippers. Dropping off the side of the boat, they swam a dozen metres to the reef, admiring teeming fish of all colours and sizes: big lethargic groupers with their thick lips, colourful angelfish trailing long dorsal fins, and schools of blue striped yellow grunts.

"What a paradise this is," Kevin marvelled. "Now I know why so many Nova Scotians come down here! Up there, you can barely swim in the ocean at the height of summer. Here, the water temperature in winter is 25 C!"

Sean had been diving to the bottom of the reef, which was only 6 feet below the surface. "There's a lobster down there who scooted into a gap in the reef when he saw me approach. I was hoping to catch my dinner, but it's not so easy, even if they don't have claws in the Bahamas!"

The dive boat took them back to the hotel in time for a walk into town. They ended up buying dinner at one of the outdoor restaurants near the commercial harbour. Sean regretted not being all alone with Amelia, but he was starting to be reconciled with the end of their relationship.

*****

Back in Ashcroft-by-the-Sea, Sean shared what they had learned from Feenstra with Hamish, who commented: "So it seems that it was indeed Francis Chastain who toned down the report given to the Summerland government."

Sean replied, "I wasn't there when they talked to him, so I didn't get a chance to ask Feenstra straight out, but it could only be him. They were at Oxford at the same time, I checked. I wonder how much he got paid to do it."

"I think I'd better make another trip to Ottawa to give Chastain the chance to explain himself. We are still no farther along however in discovering what happened to Bob Wismer and his cottage. I'm going to need to talk again to the Gatineau police inspector who is on the case."

OTTAWA AND GATINEAU, OCT. 22-24

"Mr. Cameron, this is Angela Deaver. You came by a month or so ago and I gave you Terry's papers on Summerland. Well, I found something else that may be of interest. It was at the bottom of a stack of papers in a desk drawer. It's a consultants' report prepared by APTI for the Summerland government. If you want it, you're welcome to pick it up at my house."

"Thank you. I'll stop by this afternoon, if that's all right."

"Fine, see you then."

The house in Manor Park was showing signs of lack of yard maintenance on this late fall day. The lawn had not been mowed in some time, and it was covered in places with mounds of leaves. Hamish rang the bell.

Angela opened the door and invited him in. "I've got the report on the dining table. Just let me get it."

She returned to the entranceway and handed him the report, whose front page read "Confidential Recommendations

Concerning the Proposed Ocean Pearl Casino." It was signed by Francis Chastain.

"This is very helpful, thank you," Hamish said with enthusiasm. "I've been looking for this. Do you know how Terence came to have a copy?"

"I believe that he brought this back from Balabo when he made his last trip to Summerland, since he was retiring a few months later. As desk officer for Summerland, he had some housekeeping there to do—saying goodbye to some of the officials he had dealt with, that sort of thing. He had warm relations with the people there, and they hosted a reception for him the day before he left. He said that the report was a bootleg copy. I'd forgotten all about it, but now I recall that he said he wasn't supposed to have it, but he wanted to keep it for the record."

*****

Hamish's next stop was the Gatineau police station. He was in luck, Giroux was in his office with his feet on his desk, reading through a police manual. He seemed happy for the distraction.

"Ah, the great detective! What brings you here?"

"I wanted to give you a bit of information related to the events in Summerland that I told you about, and inquire about any further developments on your side."

"OK. The only thing I found out is that Mr. Vismère claimed to be in love. That seems to be a strange thing for a man of his age to say! What do you make of that?"

"Let me first tell you what I learned. It seems that this casino built in Summerland that Wismer was looking into got conflicting advice, and that the senior person from APTI who was involved, Francis Chastain, was bribed into telling the government to go easy on law enforcement."

"Uh-oh. That makes him a suspect. Do you have any proof of this? Something that would stand up in court?"

"Probably not, but if it was made public it would destroy his reputation. He may have felt targeted by Wismer's questioning, and could have taken matters in his own hands."

"But how could he have killed Vismère? He left at midnight. Besides, there were no footprints aside from yours when I came to examine the body."

"I don't know. As for the person that Wismer was in love with, it might have been Chastain's wife, Adele. They knew each other before she married her husband, and his cottage isn't very far from hers, or rather her husband's."

"Aha, a love triangle! That gives a whole new twist to the case. I'll tell my boss that I have a new lead to follow up on! The RCMP will have to take us seriously now," he chortled.

*****

Hamish drove once again the winding road along the Gatineau River leading to Francis Chastain's house. He passed Bob Wismer's derelict cottage, and kept going for another few minutes until he could see the elegant facade of the Chastain residence through the now bare maple trees. There was no car in the driveway as he drove up.

When he rang the doorbell, it was Adele who opened it after a minute's wait. She looked startled. "Francis is not here, and I'm afraid I don't know when he'll return." She started to close the door, but Hamish raised his hand, motioning her to stop.

"It's you I wanted to see," he said, lying slightly. "Would you tell me about your relations with Bob Wismer? I know he used to be your boss, but I think he was somewhat more than that."

"What do you mean? What are you implying?" Her eyes showed anger, and she stiffened, as if to repel an attack.

"I understand that Bob Wismer claimed that he was in love with someone, and I suspect that the object of his affection was you. Isn't that true?"

"How dare you? I'm a married woman. I will not listen to such nonsense!" She stepped back, and slammed the door.

*****

Hamish showed the report to Tim Blacket. "It seems to be the definitive version of the advice given to the Summerland government. I suspect that what happened is the following. The team had some preliminary discussion of their recommendations with junior officials, then left. Apparently then Francis remained behind, staying on Harold Feenstra's yacht, and was convinced by the latter to water down the recommendations. It was Chastain's version of the proposed arrangement which was sent to the relevant cabinet minister."

"I see. And what was in the final report?"

"Whereas the APTI staff team, composed of Boudreau, Chen, and Kamara, suggested that a special police unit should be created to monitor operations of the casino, and the casino be obliged to provide the government with details of the background of its customers prior to their being admitted to Summerland, the report signed by Francis alone said that the Macau model should be adopted. That would mean that the casino would be largely self-policing. There would be no special regulations imposed on the owners, just a modest tax rate."

"So how did Francis justify that?"

"The report argued that the casino would lift economic activity in the country and hence there would be positive spill-overs on employment and government revenues through other sources, such as the value added tax on hotel room rates and restaurant meals."

"Wow! That's almost a U-turn relative to the staff position. How did Francis get away with it?"

"I don't think the staff ever learned of it, or if they did, they decided that it was in their own interest to keep quiet about it. Their work was done, and they may have assumed that their recommendations had gone to the senior government officials. But Terence Deaver, who was the desk officer and visited the country again before retiring, learned what really happened. By that time, I'm guessing, he didn't want to wake sleeping dogs."

"Why did Francis do this? Was it just to do a favour to his old pal, or was there more to it than that?"

"It's hard to know after all this time, but it seems that he was short of money, and Feenstra may well have made it very lucrative for him. Don't forget that he was wooing Adele then, after a costly divorce, and he may have felt the need to impress her with expensive presents. And he bought a sizable house in Rockcliffe shortly after their wedding."

Tim Blacket scratched his head. "How much of this can you put in a report that I will send to the board? I would just inform them of the facts, and leave it to them to decide how to proceed."

"I think the document I got from Deaver's wife speaks for itself, but I have no smoking gun that proves that Francis was bribed. Information about his finances would require police involvement. Even then, it might be impossible for them to track any financial dealings that he had with the casino's backers after two decades."

"Let's not go down that road yet. I'd like you to detail the known facts in a short report, and attach the document signed by Francis Chastain that gives the final recommendations. Then the board can summon Francis to hear what he has to say."

"Fine, I'll do that."

EASTERN UNIVERSITY, OCTOBER 30

Pamela spread her arms wide and embraced Amelia. "Welcome back to EU! I'm glad to see you safe and sound. And you're in luck, there's a free apartment in this building, so we can be neighbours again!"

"Yes, it's been a while! First Summerland, then the Bahamas. I think I have the makings of my Master's thesis, but it's not what I imagined when I left. I'm going to bounce it off Professor Fritz, assuming he'll agree once again to be my supervisor."

Professor Fritz pulled himself up to his full five-foot-eight-inch height, and gave Amelia a dressing down. "It was irresponsible of you to go off like that, you might have been jailed, or even worse! Besides, international relations is not archeology. You're not expected to do field work."

"But I did learn things I wouldn't have known if I hadn't gone to Balabo. Not only that, I met someone who was kind to me as a little kid, and now he's working once again for my father! So it all turned out well."

"So tell me, why did Summerland turn its back on the West, and is now in China's orbit? Is it a replay of the Great Game between the various European powers in the 19th and early 20th centuries?"

"Actually, no. It seems more the result of a combination of things, including the greed of one guy in a position to influence the outcome. Rather than a contest between the East and the West, the Islamic Revolution in Summerland was due to incompetence and cupidity on the part of the former government and its advisors. Moreover, the casino was as much an import from the East as from the West, since it was financed by Macau, which has since become Chinese territory. Interestingly enough, mainland China now discourages that sort of foreign investment. It is avidly pursuing Summerland's mineral deposits instead."

"Ah well, I see this will make an interesting story. I'm sure if you write it up competently you will most likely receive a Master's degree With Distinction. And you should think about getting your thesis published as a book after you receive your degree."

OTTAWA, NOVEMBER 3

The APTI board consisted of 20 directors, 10 representing the 22 donor countries and 10 representing the 54 African countries, plus APTI's president, Tim Blacket. They usually met quarterly, except when a meeting was called to deal with exceptional matters. This was one of those occasions.

Tim Blacket, the chairman of the meeting, sat at one end of the table, and Francis Chastain at the other, with ten directors on each side of the table. Senior officials of the institute attended as observers, and were seated at the sides of the room, as was Hamish.

Blacket called the meeting to order. "I expect that each of you has read the report prepared by Hamish Cameron on our activities in Summerland in the mid-1990s that was sent to you. It contains in an appendix a document listing a set of recommendations concerning the regulatory regime for a proposed casino. This was the version that was delivered to the government of Summerland by Francis Chastain. It is at odds with the report the staff team had prepared at the request of the Chinese authorities, and financed by them. Moreover, Mr. Chastain allowed his staff to accept presents over and above the remuneration they were paid by APTI as part of their work. In particular, it appears that each received a valuable pearl, and perhaps other things. I would suggest that we hear first Mr. Chastain's response to these allegations."

"Mr. Chairman, please let me interrupt," said the Chinese board member. "I would like the record to read that my government was not aware of the recommendations signed by Mr. Chastain that are before us today. Instead, we were given a different document that recommended a much more restrictive regime for the casino, and safeguards to make sure that criminal elements did not use the casino for their illicit activities. Until now, we believed that those were the final recommendations and that they were the ones presented to the Summerland government."

"Thank you, Mr. Lee. Now, Mr. Chastain, would you please explain how there came to be two sets of recommendations concerning the casino in Summerland?"

Francis Chastain sat stiffly in his chair, his hands clasped rigidly in front of him. "Our terms of reference instructed us to consult with the stakeholders in Summerland before preparing our final report. Therefore, we first discussed our draft report with government officials to get their reaction. As a next step, I met with the backers of the casino from Macau. They told me categorically that they would not be able to operate at a profit under the conditions specified in our draft report. Since I knew that the government had made a commitment to build the casino, I judged that the report as it stood would not serve any useful purpose. Since my team had already departed Summerland, and the deadline for the final report was rapidly approaching, I took it upon myself to modify the recommendations so that they aligned more closely with the regulations then in place in Macau."

The Chinese director spoke up once again. "Mr. Chastain, I would like to point out that the regulatory regime in Macau has since been made considerably stricter. Moreover, other jurisdictions such as the United States, Monaco, and the United Kingdom, have more restrictions on the operation of casinos than those you recommended for Summerland."

"Are there other comments by directors? If not, then I would like to turn to another topic and ask Mr. Chastain whether he or his staff received any remuneration or gifts from the stakeholders of the casino?"

Chastain's face showed his displeasure with the question. "Mr. Chairman, we were each given a present by the Minister as an expression of the government's gratitude for the work that we had undertaken. It would have been churlish for us to refuse the gift of a pearl, symbol of the country. I am not familiar with the value of pearls we were given, but I have always assumed that they have ceremonial, rather than monetary, value."

"You accepted, and allowed staff to accept, those presents despite APTI's rules that forbid staff from accepting remuneration in addition to their usual salaries?"

"The work undertaken for Summerland was financed by the country funds, and I had concluded that my team was not bound by the staff rules in this case. It was just a token present anyway, not a form of remuneration."

The directors around the table questioned this assertion. The Chinese board member, in particular, was very critical of Chastain's actions. He condemned the decision to modify the staff's report–paid for by the Chinese government–and not to inform his authorities or the APTI board.

Blacket as chairman read a summary of the discussion, prepared by a staff member who had taken notes, to close the meeting. "Directors pushed back against the suggestion that work financed by country funds was not bound by the usual regulations. They emphasized the need to obey staff rules in all circumstances and condemned the laxity that was evident in the work for Summerland directed by Francis Chastain. They concluded that studies undertaken at the request of individual countries, such as that financed by the Chinese authorities in the case of Summerland, should be discussed by the entire board, which would be called to give its approval before their release."

The board's decision was a clear criticism of Francis Chastain's actions. While no sanction was imposed on him, it was obvious that he was no longer considered an emeritus retiree of the institution.

As the participants filed out of the board room, Chastain glared at Hamish, but did not say a word.

*****

Hamish recounted what had happened at APTI's board meeting to Jessica Bowles over dinner at an Italian restaurant on O'Connor Street, once a favourite of Hamish's. The food now was so-so, but eating at this particular restaurant, which had been in business for a long time, was nostalgic for both of them.

Jessica interrupted. "I actually heard what happened through the grapevine. You know news travels fast in Ottawa. I gather that Francis got his knuckles rapped."

"You could say so. His defence was pretty lame, and there were no directors there willing to take his side. The Chinese director was especially damning, making it very clear that his authorities had no part in or knowledge of his lobbying for the casino backers. Moreover, they were dismayed that Chastain had presented recommendations to the Summerland government without informing them, though the Chinese had financed the project. So he was left hanging out to dry."

"I'm guessing that any hope he had of appearing on the Queen's Birthday Honours List is gone."

"You can say that again! And I think that the Gatineau police are now looking carefully at his possible involvement in Bob's death and the torching of his cottage."

"So are you still involved in investigating those? I'm guessing that APTI has wrapped up their inquiry, and don't want any more from you."

"Yes, that's true. They would rather I would now just leave things as they are. But Bob Wismer was a friend, and what happened to him shouldn't be forgotten. I'm still convinced that there was an element of foul play, and whoever did it should be held accountable for it. I'm not sure the Gatineau police will find out what happened. What do you think I should do?"

Jessica brushed his cheek with her hand. "I think you should keep investigating, if only because it means that I will see more of you!" She smiled and gave him a knowing look.

"I wish you'd talk again with Adele. I'd bet that she's the reason that Francis did what he did in Summerland. But I think that their marriage is coming apart now, and that Bob was the reason for that."

"I'll invite her to lunch. Now that she and I have linked up again, it won't seem out of place. If it's just the two of us, then maybe she'll confide in me. I'll let you know."

GATINEAU AND OTTAWA, NOV. 4-5

The inspector rang the doorbell at the Chastain mansion on the Gatineau River and waited impatiently in the glacial wind for someone to open the door. He wasn't sure that there was still someone staying there, since it was late in the season. *Maybe I'll have to visit them at their Rockcliffe house. I hope not, since I'll have to liaise with the Ottawa police. Tabarnouche! I don't want that!*

Finally the door opened a crack, and a woman looked out questioningly.

"Brrr. Can I come in? Are you Mrs. Chastain?" He showed her his police identification.

"That's right. But what do you want?" She didn't open the door more widely.

"I'd like to talk to you about the events that took place at Bob Vismère's cottage in September—just for background."

"Oh, very well. But I thought this was settled a long time ago." She quickly shut the door to keep out the cold wind after he ducked inside. "Please come into the living room."

Giroux admired the view over the deck, especially now that the trees had lost their leaves so he could see a good way down the river. "You can almost see Mr. Vismère's cottage from here, can't you? Did you visit him often?"

Adele frowned. "Why do you ask?"

"I'm trying to understand his relations with you and your husband. Do you think he was trying to blackmail Mr. Chastain? After all, Vismère brought up this business in Summerland at the retirement party for him. Could that be the reason for his death?"

"That's nonsense. Francis would never do that! Besides, Bob's death was an accident." She bit her tongue. "I mean, that was the conclusion everyone reached, wasn't it? Why are you looking into it now?"

"We need to close the case, once and for all. We are following up all the leads. I gather you worked for Mr. Vismère at the Institute—what's its name, APTI—before you married your husband. Is that right?"

"Yes, that's right. So what? What are you implying?"

"Just that you would have a good reason to see him, on, say, a social basis," he said with a smile curling his lips.

Furious, Adele marched to the front door, and, oblivious to the cold, she held it open and shouted. "Out! I will not answer any more of your questions!"

Reluctantly, Giroux got up from his chair, and walked slowly to the door. Without a word, he stepped outside, got into his car shivering, and drove off.

*****

"I don't know why they are still pawing through Bob's activities," Adele said to Jessica. They were having a light lunch at a new eatery off Sussex Drive, near the Byward Market. "I mean, what do they hope to learn?"

"You're right, it seems settled that his death was an accident. But I guess they're still trying to discover who started the fire, since they've concluded it was arson."

Adele turned away, and poked around in her purse for a throat lozenge. "I'm getting a sore throat from this cold weather. Francis may have caught something as well. That APTI board meeting he went to didn't help his humour or his health!"

"I heard about the reprimand he received. How is he taking it?"

"Not too well. He sees everything he accomplished there as being washed away by the events in Summerland. He's going to go to his grave a bitter man."

"Did he actually get some compensation from the casino owners for his cooperation, or just a token present from the government?" Jessica noticed that Adele was not wearing the pearl necklace today.

Adele looked away. "I'd rather not talk about it, if you don't mind. Francis is honest and upright, and I can't see him being bribed," she said primly.

Jessica, seeing Adele's reaction, realized that she had gone too far, so she changed the subject. "I heard from Bob's lawyer today that I'll receive a small legacy from his estate. Most of it goes to his son, of course. He was a dear friend, though that was a long time ago. We should organize a memorial service for him. What do you think?"

"That's a good idea. I miss him."

The server arrived with their food, causing them to break off their conversation.

They chatted about other things throughout the meal, and said goodbye with a hug before going their separate ways.

When Jessica got to her car, she noticed that she no longer had her sunglasses. *Damn, I must have left them at the restaurant.* While she was heading back, she saw Adele up ahead walking next to a man and talking animatedly. Jessica lagged behind, curious about who it was but not wanting to appear nosy. So far, neither Adele nor the man had looked behind them. As they crossed a street, the man checked to make sure there was no traffic and Jessica saw his face. *It's Roger Boudreau. My, my, my, Adele certainly gets around!*

They were walking away from the restaurant now. Jessica retrieved her sunglasses without being seen by them and drove back to her office on Sussex Drive.

When she got a free moment during her afternoon crowded with meetings, she called Hamish and told him about seeing Adele and Roger together. "Do you think they've kept in touch since they were both at APTI two decades ago? Or is it a recent thing, since Bob passed away?"

"Roger told me he's doing some contract work in francophone Africa for Global Affairs, and he has to come to Ottawa periodically to report. This must have started after he retired from the French aid agency, so I'm guessing he's only recently linked up with Adele. Can you do another thing for me? Since you also work on Africa at GAC, it should be easy for you to find out who he reports to and how often he comes to Ottawa."

"Sure, I can do that for you, Hamish."

OTTAWA, NOVEMBER 6

"Clarence, this is Hamish Cameron again. I have another question: were you aware that there was another report that was personally delivered to the Summerland government by Francis Chastain? It was used as justification for subjecting the casino to very light regulation."

"No, this is news to me! Why would he do something like that?"

"It seems that he was talked into it by his old Oxford pal, Sir Harold Feenstra–the backer of the casino. Maybe he was generously compensated, too."

"If I'd known, I would have spoken up about Francis's role on the Ocean Pearl project at his retirement party. I'm very disappointed. This is a man I admired, but I can't say I do any more."

"I hear you. Did he say anything to you and the others when he came back from Summerland?

"No, he didn't say a word, but I remember that he had a new bounce in his step. What you said may explain it: with the money he got in Summerland he could go ahead and marry Adele. He would be able to cater to her expensive tastes."

"Do you remember whether Roger Boudreau was also interested in Adele at the time?"

Chen shrugged his shoulders. "I think a lot of men were, and she played the field. Roger was single then, and I'll bet they dated at some point. How serious it was, I don't know. As for Bob, I don't think he had any romantic relationship with Adele while she was working for him. But that may have changed later, for all I know."

*****

"I heard you were in Ottawa, Roger, so I thought I would try to get hold of you to see if you wanted to meet for a drink. I'm staying at the Marriott on Kent Street. How about you?"

"Oh, hello Hamish. I'm just here for another day, but, pourquoi pas, let's meet at your hotel. How about in an hour, at 5 o'clock?"

Hamish had been waiting for 15 minutes when Roger walked into the ground floor bar. He was dressed in slacks and a knit shirt, so Hamish guessed that he had not come directly from meetings at Global Affairs. They exchanged greetings and Roger ordered a Kronenbourg beer.

Roger started by asking, "Have you heard anything about the Gatineau police investigation? They haven't got in touch with me since I left Bob's cottage. I heard about the fire the next day, though. You weren't hurt, I hope? I think you were still staying there?"

"Yes, I was the one who reported the fire. I had just returned from dinner with Jessica. The fire department concluded that it was arson, which has led the police to keep the case of Bob's death open. As far as I know, they don't have any evidence that it was murder but that's still a possibility."

"Oh, I see." Roger frowned. "I thought they had ruled that out when the inspector examined the scene."

"They're struggling to find a motive. I suggested to Inspector Giroux that it might be related to Bob's poking into what happened in Summerland. Since then I've learned that Francis ignored the report that you, John, and Clarence prepared, and recommended that the casino be given a free rein."

"He did what? Oh, so you know that we worked on a report paid for by China. We told them that they should beef up their supervision and make sure organized crime didn't get a foothold. So Francis undercut our work? Well, well ..." Boudreau looked furious.

"The board has given him a reprimand. I think that ends APTI's investigation of the events in Summerland. But if you and the others had still been working at APTI, you might have faced sanctions."

"You realize that it was Francis who volunteered us to do the work. We were just following his orders. Anyway, thank you for letting me know. I'll be sure to avoid having any dealings with APTI in the future."

"I wanted to ask you about something else that happened when we were at Bob's cottage. I seem to remember that you were awake around the time of the storm. Did you hear anything?"

"What do you mean?"

"We heard from Clarence that there might have been a car that stopped at Bob's cottage in the early hours of the morning, but he didn't know if it was before or after the storm. But the lack of footprints outside suggest that he went out before, or during, the storm, not afterwards. It was then that he died. You might have heard him leaving the house, and, if so, when?"

Roger gave it some thought before answering. "It's true that I heard some shuffling around, and I assumed it was Bob straightening up the house. But I didn't hear any door opening or closing, so I don't know if he or someone else went in or out. So I can't shed any light on what happened."

"Do you have any theories?"

"No, I don't have a clue! I suppose Francis was unhappy with Bob's scrutiny of the work on Summerland's casino, but I hardly think he would go so far as murdering him!"

"How about the possibility that Bob was romantically involved with Adele, and Francis was aware of it. Would that incite him to murder?"

Roger looked startled. "Bob and Adele? That's a far-fetched reason for murder! My guess is that Francis is reconciled to the fact that his much younger wife is going to flirt with men closer to her own age. Like Lord Hamilton when his wife was the companion of Horatio Nelson!"

"So you can't come up with any motive for Bob's murder?"

"No, I can't believe that it was murder."

OTTAWA AND GATINEAU, NOV. 7-8

Hamish was in bed about to go to sleep when his cell phone rang. "Monsieur Cameronne? It's Inspecteur Giroux. Sorry to bother you at this time of night, but there's been another death. It's Francis Chastain. He was found at the foot of the steps that lead to his dock. Like the other one, he has a wound to his head."

Hamish sat up abruptly. "That's terrible! Another death–what in heaven's name is going on?"

Giroux asked quickly: "Do you want to come and have a look?"

Hamish hesitated for a moment. "I'll come, but not before tomorrow morning when there's enough light to see. In the meantime, I assume you've talked to the widow? What story does she tell about what happened?"

"OK, meet me at my office on Boulevard Gréber as early as you can and I'll drive you there. I've looked at the steps leading down to the water and there's nothing. No footprints, nothing. The widow says she doesn't know why he was outside, but thinks that he must have slipped."

"See you tomorrow morning."

Hamish mused that Giroux must be desperate for clues to call him. *Another possible murder, and he hasn't solved the first one. His boss must really be on his back.*

He snuggled under the covers. At least I'll be able to get my eight hours of sleep tonight. If I don't, then I'm of no use at all!

*****

Adele Chastain was sitting in the living room looking out over the river. Her face was stained with tears. She nodded stiffly to the two men. "What more do you want to ask? I told you everything I knew last night."

"Mais oui, Madame. I understand. But I would like to go over that again with my colleague here." He gave a nod to Hamish. "He's helping in the investigation."

"What investigation? It's clear what happened, it was an accident!"

"We have to go through the formalities, especially since there have been two unfortunate accidents along the river in the space of two months. Now, when did you discover the body?"

"I didn't see him around the house, so I went out onto the deck to look in the yard. It was about eight o'clock. We'd finished dinner an hour before. It was dark, but the spotlights were turned on so I could make out someone lying on the ground near the river. I ran down the path and saw that it was my husband. I called 911 right away."

Giroux scratched his head. "Why would he have gone down the path? There's nothing at the dock."

"I don't know."

"Did you have any visitors during the afternoon or evening?"

"No, we were the only ones here."

Hamish interjected. "Was your husband depressed? Could he have thrown himself off the deck?"

"He wasn't happy as a result of the board meeting at APTI, but I wouldn't say he was depressed. Certainly not to the point of doing that." Adele took up the handkerchief in her lap and dabbed her eyes.

Giroux got up. "That's all for now, Madame, though we may need to talk to you again. You have my condolences for your loss. My men will continue to search outside, but I will make sure they do not bother you." The two men left by the door from the living room to the deck.

Hamish looked carefully at the glass barrier around it. It was about 4 feet high. The frost showed recent fingerprints on the steel railing at a point above the place where the body had been found, but no other marks. "I assume you've taken photos of those prints?"

Giroux shrugged. "Of course. We will compare them with those of the victim and his wife."

They descended toward the river. "Here is where he was found," Giroux explained, pointing to a spot near to the dock and at the bottom of the steep hill leading down from the house. The weather had turned cold, and there was some ice on the steps of the path that curved around in a half circle from the back door down to the water.

Hamish looked up toward the deck, which was directly above. "I wonder if he fell off the deck, rather than from the path. If he had slipped on the path, he wouldn't have ended up here. Is there any indication of where he landed?" he asked the inspector.

"I didn't want to disturb the area in the dark. I'll get one of my men to examine the area carefully now."

"How badly was his head injured? Did he hit a rock, or just hit the ground? If he fell from the deck, which is 20 metres above the river, he could have died from the concussion, even if he landed on the ground."

"Ah, yes, I see. The coroner's report should tell us that when we get it. In the meantime, we'll start by looking along a straight line from the deck to where he was found." Giroux gave instructions to one of his men.

On the way back to police headquarters, he asked Hamish: "So what do you think?"

"It looks like an accident, just like Bob Wismer's death. But can it be a coincidence that there are two of them so close together? I don't know. What was Chastain doing? Like Wismer, we don't know why he was outside. Maybe he was meeting someone. But who?"

"It's too bad there's no security camera." Giroux thought for a moment. "Or is there?" He braked suddenly, then made a U-turn and sped back toward the Chastain residence. "I remember now. There was an alarm company sticker by the front door. I'd expect them to put cameras around the house. Let's see who it is and call them."

When they reached the house Giroux made a note of the name and number of the alarm company. Before leaving once again he checked with the policeman he had charged with searching the hill below the deck. "Find anything?"

"Oui, chef, the ground half-way down the hill seems to have been flattened, maybe by a body. We'll see if there are any DNA traces."

"OK, keep looking."

*****

Giroux called the alarm company from his car on the way back to Boulevard Gréber. Their office was in Ottawa, and the security camera recordings were available for the Chastain residence. "We'll head over to Heron Road directly, if that's OK with you," Giroux asked Hamish. "We need to look at the camera footage as soon as possible."

They were shown into the office of Ravi Malek, who was the manager. "We keep recordings for only a day, then they are overwritten by new footage in a 24 hour loop. Our staff only monitors them if an alarm goes off at the site. If there's evidence of a break-in on the video then the police are alerted. After you called, I saved the last 24 hours in a separate file so it won't get overwritten." He motioned for them to look at his computer monitor as he fast forwarded the video, which displayed a time in the top right corner.

"Why don't you start at 7:30 pm yesterday, and go from there," Giroux suggested.

They stared at the screen, which displayed all six cameras' recordings simultaneously. At first, all showed an unchanging picture as Malek scrolled through. Then, at about 8 pm, Adele was seen coming onto the deck. She leaned against the railing, and looked down. Startled by what she'd seen, she ran down the path. She could dimly be seen bending over something below.

"*Merde*, we need to start earlier, say at 6:30 pm."

At 7 pm Francis Chastain walked out the front door and strolled around the driveway. He seemed to be waiting for something, with his hands in his pockets. A few minutes later a car pulled up, and Chastain walked to the driver's side. The driver was not visible through the tinted windshield, but the two seemed to be talking. Chastain started to shake his head. Waving his hands, he turned his back and walked around the house toward the deck in back. As he reached it, the man in the car jumped out and slammed into Francis, projecting him down the hill.

Hamish gasped. "It's Boudreau. He pushed Chastain over the cliff! Why did he do this?"

The man ran to his car and drove off.

"*Ciboire*, I'll need you to give me a copy of that video right now. Hamish, come with me, I'm going to make a call from the police car to arrest Boudreau, if he's still in town. I'll get them to broadcast it to all police units and to the border agents."

GATINEAU, NOVEMBER 9

While the search was on for Roger Boudreau, Giroux and Cameron returned to the Chastain residence to speak to Adele. She let them in after a wait of several minutes. She was dishevelled, and without makeup, wearing the same house dress as when they interviewed her earlier.

Giroux explained why they had returned. "We've obtained the surveillance camera video from your alarm company. I'm sorry to have to inform you that your husband was pushed down the slope by Roger Boudreau. He must have hit the ground with such force that it killed him."

Adele put her hands beside her face, and shook her head in disbelief. "Oh, no! Why would Roger do that?"

"That's what we wanted to ask you. Did you know he was coming to visit? Did you talk to him at all?"

"I ran into him yesterday near the Byward Market. I had lunch with a woman I used to know at APTI, and then I saw him walking along the street while I was returning to my car.

We chatted a bit, but that was all. I had no idea he would come by here. He didn't mention Francis either."

Hamish added for both Adele's and Giroux's benefit: "I had a drink with Roger at my hotel at the end of the afternoon. I told him that Francis had gone behind his back and submitted a report to the Summerland government that gave the casino a blank cheque. He didn't seem happy at all. That may have set him off. He must have called Francis, because it's clear from the video that your husband was expecting someone. Francis may have offered to explain, but he couldn't convince Roger."

Adele nodded. "That could be. I heard the phone ring but I don't know who called or what was said."

"Did your husband see Roger often? Apparently, Roger comes to Ottawa fairly frequently." Hamish looked fixedly at Adele.

"I don't think so. As far as I know, when they met at Bob's party they hadn't seen each other for a long time."

"I see. Can you tell us anything else about the party, or what Bob was doing down by the water when he died? I don't think the inspector had a chance to interview you at the time." He turned toward Giroux, who shook his head.

Adele squirmed in her chair. "I have a confession to make. I made a visit to Bob's cottage by boat at around 2 o'clock in the morning. My husband had come back from the party very upset that Bob was looking into the Summerland casino project. He asked me to try to talk him out of it. He knew that we were friends, so he thought I could convince him. I often took the skiff to visit Bob at night when Francis was asleep. When I got to his dock and was about to tie up to it, I saw that he was floating in the water, dead. It was awful, but there was nothing I could do." She sobbed.

"Why didn't you call the police?"

"It was too late to save Bob, and I was afraid of the scandal. I would have had to explain that Bob and I were lovers. Francis didn't know, or didn't want to know. If it became public he would feel obliged to retaliate against me. I didn't want a divorce. So I went back to our cottage and went to bed."

Adele continued: "The next day Francis learned that Bob had been found drowned. He was the one who went back in the evening to set fire to Bob's cottage. He was afraid there might be incriminating documents related to Summerland in there."

Hamish nodded his head. "So that's what happened! Luckily I had taken Bob's papers on Summerland with me. They were in the trunk of my car."

Giroux was incredulous. "So Madame Chastain, you're saying that you found a dead body, and your husband set fire to his house, but you had nothing to do with it? That's hard to swallow! And now another body, that of your husband!"

Adele covered her face with her hands in order to hide her tears. "It's true, I swear!"

"I need to caution you that you are a suspect in a murder case."

Adele shook her head. "I'm not saying anything more! I've told you what I know. I'm innocent."

Giroux tried to calm her. "We're not accusing you of anything yet, Madame, but we will be pursuing the investigation. We're done for now, but we will want a detailed statement later. Please feel free to contact your lawyer."

OTTAWA AND GATINEAU, NOV. 10

When Roger Boudreau came down from his room carrying his suitcase, two members of the Ottawa police force were waiting for him in the lobby. He hesitated, looked around, and came to the conclusion that he had no way to evade them.

One of the officers approached him. "Mr. Boudreau? You are accused of the murder of Francis Chastain. You have the right to remain silent and to retain and instruct counsel."

He did not say a word, and did not resist when the officer put handcuffs on him. He was taken to Boulevard Gréber at Inspector Giroux's request. In the meantime, Boudreau had contacted a solicitor, who briefly conferred with him before the two of them entered the interrogation room.

Giroux was flanked by one of his deputies on the other side of a table in the otherwise unfurnished room. Invited by Giroux, Hamish was standing outside and looking through a one-way window at the suspect. A speaker allowed him to listen to the interview.

Boudreau's solicitor turned to Giroux and said: "My client would like to make a statement."

Boudreau was ashen, but seemed determined to defend himself. He read from a piece of paper that he had prepared with the help of his solicitor. "I visited Francis Chastain yesterday because I learned that he had gone behind the backs of my colleagues and me by giving contrary advice to the government of Summerland when we tried to protect the country from the crime that the establishment of a casino could bring. I phoned him to protest, but he refused to discuss it. Reluctantly, he agreed to explain his actions if I came to see him at his cottage. So I drove my rental car from the hotel to his place on the Gatineau River. His defence was that our report would have been rejected out of hand, so that he felt compelled to give more realistic recommendations, as he called them. I told him that was nonsense, and that he had just been acting as the mouthpiece of the casino owners. He started to get angry at me, threatening to denounce me to Global Affairs Canada so that they would no longer employ me, and accusing me of sleeping with his wife, which was a lie. He shouted that he didn't give a damn anyway about what had happened in Summerland. I told him that he was a fraud. He had worked for an organization dedicated to helping African countries but instead had betrayed them. He rushed toward the back of his house, yelling that he would get his shotgun. I was a sitting duck because I would have had to back my car up and manoeuvre around his SUV, so I jumped out of my vehicle and tackled him from behind. I hadn't realized that the hill was so steep. He went over the edge. I didn't wait around to see if he was all right, but instead I drove away."

Boudreau's solicitor announced that his client would not take any questions. The interview was over.

An officer took Boudreau to a holding cell, while Hamish and the inspector went back to his desk. The latter said to Hamish: "I guess this closes the case. Boudreau can plead manslaughter. We know who torched the cottage, and Vismère's death was an accident, as I thought all along."

"So you think that Bob was meeting Adele, slipped and hit his head; then he rolled into the water and drowned? He just happened to do all this just before Adele got there. I guess it's plausible, but there are other possible scenarios."

"Oh, yeah? Like what?"

"We still have the same suspects that we had before for Bob's murderer, if his death was indeed murder."

"And who are they?"

"Everyone who was at the party, and perhaps Adele as well. The key is to find a motive. We had a motive for Chastain, but it was difficult, if not impossible, for him to have had the opportunity. But one of the remaining guests at the cottage could have slipped out of the house when Bob went to meet Adele and murdered him. Or she could have done so herself."

"But why?"

"Exactly. We don't have a plausible motive. But I think Bob had something else that he hoped to reveal in the book he was writing. He said to Jessica Bowles that it would be 'explosive.' I don't think the team's report to the Summerland government quite qualifies for that description. Unfortunately, with the fire we don't have much of a chance of finding what Bob had in his possession."

"So I go back to what I said before. The case is closed. Maybe Bob's death was a murder, but we have no evidence of that, and we're not going to find it. *Ite missa est.* Amen."

Hamish shook his head. "I'm not so sure. I'd like to look into some more loose ends."

ASHCROFT, NOVEMBER 30

Sean had concluded that his brief affair with Amelia was over. She was half his age. It could never work. He plunged himself into other activities.

First on his list was getting some work done on his house before the onset of winter. The hot water heating was once again not working the way it should, and one of the pipes leading to the radiators on the third floor was leaking. Sean had turned off the heat and was shivering as he contemplated what to do. *I probably should replace all the pipes, which are at least a hundred years old, or junk the hot water heating system and just put in electric baseboard heaters. Installing ducts for forced air would require ripping the walls apart! Whatever I do, it's going to soak up a lot of money!*

The ringing of the phone interrupted his discouraging thoughts. "Hello, Sean Carroll here."

"Hello Sean, this is Richard Owens calling from Macau. I kept your card so I knew how to contact you. I have another piece to the puzzle of what happened in Summerland."

Sean answered warmly. "Oh, is that right? It's nice of you to take the trouble to call. What have you learned, exactly?"

"Well, you asked me what triggered the coup d'état, and I didn't really have a good answer. Now I think I do. You remember that I mentioned that Sir Harold Feenstra was one of our big investors? Well, he also owns a company, Xanadu Mining, that's starting to exploit Summerland's vast lithium deposits, which are especially valuable now that everyone wants to turn away from fossil fuels and go to electric vehicles. The Summerland government has given Xanadu a monopoly over lithium extraction there."

"OK. But how does this relate to the coup in 1998?"

"Well, back then, one of your countrymen had control of those deposits, though he wasn't actually exploiting them. Feenstra had the foresight to realize that they would be very valuable one day. But he had no way of getting a hold of them. They were on land that Truro Resources owned, and on which it mined other minerals, so it didn't want to sell. He no doubt hoped that if a new regime was put in place, it could be induced to take back the concessions granted to Truro Resources. Feenstra would bide his time and eventually make a play for the mining rights to the lithium when the country was ready to open up again. "

"So Feenstra engineered a coup to get at them?" Sean's tone emphasized his incredulity.

"Actually, that was only part of the reason. Because the casino wasn't making money, he wanted to get out of that investment. But he wouldn't have been able to sell his holding; no one would buy it given its meagre returns. Instead, he saw a change of regime as a way to get his insurance to compensate him for losses on that investment. He was insured for expropriation risk, and a takeover of the casino would trigger it. "

"So did that work out according to plan? How did he manage to provoke a change of regime?"

"He deliberately made the casino staff work during Ramadan, in order to foment opposition to the casino and the existing government. Probably he did not anticipate that it would actually lead to its overthrow, just that it would mean that the casino would be closed and he would be able to make an insurance claim. But his plan succeeded amazingly well, and the new Islamic regime quickly closed the casino and rescinded the mining rights of all foreign companies."

"But how did Feenstra manage to have those rights given to Xanadu?"

"He hired an insider to get the concessions granted to his company when the time was ripe. Feenstra was willing to wait as long as necessary for the country to open up again. He knew that eventually they would want to exploit their mineral resources, and when they did, he would make a good return on his investment."

"Who was that?"

"Someone called Clarence Chen. He was not exactly an insider, but he was someone who had extensive contacts in Summerland and knowledge of the mining business. He had met with Feenstra and impressed him with his ability to make things happen. He was ethnically Chinese, so he had no trouble convincing the Chinese authorities that he was on their side. As a result of his work on the casino proposal, he had met with many of the Summerland officials. So he had contacts in the right places. He helped instigate further opposition to the casino. He convinced the people in the civil service whom he knew that the casino was corrupting the country. Far from opposing Francis Chastain's recommendations to put in place a lax regulatory regime for the casino, Chen supported them because they would fan the flames of the Islamic outrage.

"After the coup, Chen gradually refreshed his contacts with those who were now serving the new regime. He bided his time until the regime saw that it couldn't go it alone and needed partners. Chen paved the way for a Chinese backed mining company to be given a monopoly on mineral exploitation in Summerland. Thanks to him, Xanadu Mining has been given sole access to the country's minerals. And in the meantime, with Macau having become a Chinese territory, Feenstra forged a pact with the Chinese to use his company as a conduit for Chinese resource development."

"And why would he do that?"

"Feenstra had no choice if he wanted to stay in Macau, where he is heavily invested. Otherwise, the Chinese Communist Party would have squeezed him out and he would have lost what he had painstakingly built. As it was, they let in the Vegas casinos, taking away business from the empire built by Stanley Ho. Feenstra would have been forced to sell his casino holdings at bargain-basement prices. And I don't think he would want to go back to the UK and face the taxation there."

"Sounds like a plausible story, but how did you learn of it?"

"I have a friend in Summerland from my casino days. He works at the Mining Commission. He's been shepherding the country's vast lithium deposits, and resents the influence that

Chen has acquired over the country's resource policies. He gave me this information because he hopes to reverse the decision giving Xanadu control of the mineral deposits. I can't give you his name, for obvious reasons."

*****

Hamish paced back and forth in the detective agency's office, located in what was once a dining room in Sean's family mansion. "So Chen would have been scared of what Bob Wismer's investigation into Summerland would turn up. He might have been exposed as a Chinese agent, and he also risked losing the rewards from having steered Summerland's lithium deposits China's way. I suspect that they would have been enormous! He would go from being a mediocrely paid professor to a mover and shaker who could rival Sir Harold's wealth and influence. This would have provided a powerful motive to shut Bob Wismer up!"

Sean shook his head. "But there's no proof that Bob's death was murder. Even if it was a murder, you can't prove he did it. Discovering a motive is all very good, but where's the evidence that he committed it?"

"You're right. But maybe we can get proof. Here's what I have in mind …"

OTTAWA,
DECEMBER 1

Hamish looked over at Clarence Chen. They were on the rooftop terrace of a building near to where he had his office. Since it was a nice sunny early winter day, Chen had suggested that they go up there. "Thanks for seeing me once again, Clarence. I gather you're quite busy. Are you teaching here at Carleton University, or just doing your own research?"

"I'm on sabbatical from the National University of Singapore, and I'm writing a book that I need to finish by the end of the year for my publisher, World Scientific."

"Are you almost done? What's the subject? "

"It's on the management of natural resources in Africa, which takes many different forms and involves many complications. In some countries, the ownership of these resources is left to sub-national regions; in others, it's the national government that owns them. Nigeria is a country where a war broke out between the federal government and one of the states over this issue. Even your own country, Canada, sees conflicts between the resource-rich provinces and the national government. Another issue is whether exhaustible resources should be treated like any other revenue source or instead saved. Some governments create a natural resources fund for future generations with the proceeds so that they can continue to benefit from them after the resources have been depleted, while others just funnel resource revenues into the budget. It's a fascinating patchwork of institutional mechanisms, some more effective in building the country's wealth than others. African countries, sadly, are prime examples of the 'curse of oil'. Natural resource exploitation, far from adding to national prosperity, often leads to corruption, strife, and the abandonment of otherwise profitable activities such as agriculture and manufacturing."

"I guess your work on Summerland at APTI must have stimulated your interest in the subject. Natural resources were a big contributor to that country's foreign earnings, at least until the revolution."

Chen looked wary. "That's true. Though I only had a limited involvement there, only looking at the casino project. And that was a long time ago."

"Something you denied until you were confronted with the truth. And now you deny that you were involved with natural resources there. But you were seen in the Mining Commission offices recently. How do you explain that?"

Chen bridled. "I don't have to explain anything to you! But I will tell you why: I was researching my book, and I didn't want to leave out Summerland from the study, even though it has few resources when compared to its neighbours."

"That's not quite true, is it? With the demand for lithium there is now, and prices going way up, any country with substantial deposits like Summerland's is going to see a boom in mining to rival the gold rush! How much are the Chinese paying you to get a monopoly for Xanadu Mining?"

"Now wait a minute! You can't barge in and make these unfounded allegations. I'm going to ask you to leave, right now! If you don't, I'm calling the campus police."

"I wouldn't do that if I were you. Contrary to what you say, the allegations are in fact backed up by people in the Summerland government who know what they're talking about. And I think that you murdered Bob Wismer because you realized that if he continued to dig up information about the casino he would eventually find you out."

"That's ridiculous! I had nothing to do with that! We shared a bedroom at the cottage, so you know I didn't get up until much later. I couldn't have killed Bob. Anyway, the police have said it was an accident." Chen was getting increasingly excited.

"I thought so too, because you were in bed and seemingly asleep when I got up around 1:30 am. Your story about waking up when your sleeping pills' effect wore off made sense, but, in fact, you murdered him before you went to bed. I went out like a light, and I didn't see or hear you come in. You must have stayed downstairs to talk to Bob, to sound him out, after the rest of us went upstairs. When you realized that he was on your trail, you lured him outside and hit him with a rock. You pushed him into the water, and left the stone on the shore. The storm, when it came through, erased your footprints and his. Your story of hearing someone stopping by later was meant to deflect blame onto others, should the police suspect murder."

"That's preposterous! You made all this up, and you've not got one tiny bit of proof!"

"Don't be too sure of that! In any case, once Sir Harold Feenstra hears that you are being investigated for murder, he's going to drop you like the bad apple that you are. You won't be of any further use to him, or to the Chinese. Your hopes of winning the jackpot will be gone."

They were now close to the edge of the rooftop terrace atop the building. Chen let out a roar and pushed Hamish upwards and over the railing. Desperately trying to grab something, Hamish snagged the bottom of the railing with both hands, just able to pull his body up onto the narrow ledge that was between the railing and the ten-story drop to the ground. As Chen was about to kick at Hamish's hands on the railing to dislodge them, Inspecteur Giroux emerged from the stairway.

"Stop right there! You're under arrest!" A policeman who had been following behind Giroux ran over to Chen, grabbed his arms and cuffed him. He did not offer any resistance.

Giroux rushed over to the railing. He seized Hamish by the shoulders and helped him get back to safety. Hamish's hands were trembling from the exertion of holding on. His face was bruised from scraping it on the stone ledge.

"That was a close one! I expected him to give something away, but not to assault me. He's stronger than he looks!"

"Yes, we have him on attempted murder now. We'll review Vismère's death again in the light of this, and search Chen's office and apartment. I expect we'll find something."

OTTAWA, DECEMBER 2

Jessica dabbed at Hamish's face with a tissue. "You look as though you've been through the wars! How does it feel? Shouldn't you see a doctor?"

"Oh, it doesn't hurt too much. It's just a superficial scrape. Much less painful I'm sure than falling 10 stories!"

"So, you're done with Ottawa and APTI now?"

"Yes, except for testifying at the trial if I'm needed. Giroux has found one of the missing reports on the Summerland casino in Chen's apartment, the one that was supposedly delivered to the Summerland government but was replaced by Chastain's version. He also had some correspondence from the Chinese authorities that makes it clear he was working for them. He is going to be charged with murdering Bob Wismer. Since he is also accused of attempted manslaughter, with Giroux and his deputy as witnesses, in addition to me, he's almost certain to be ending his days in prison."

"How did you figure out that Chen was the culprit? From the beginning, the police didn't think it was murder at all, just an unfortunate accident given the slippery steps down to the water."

"Chen was unlucky that Chastain set fire to Bob's cottage. That made both me and the police suspicious. It seemed likely that Bob's death and the arson were related, and they were–but not in the way we thought. They weren't caused by the same person, though they were both related to long-ago events in Summerland."

"You were suspicious of Chastain all along, though."

"Not at first. I still remembered the distinguished lawyer I had worked under decades before. But he was so evasive it made me think that he was implicated in some way. He changed his story each time he was confronted with questions, or he was so vague it made me wonder what he was hiding. The behaviour of the three who worked on the report–Boudreau, Chen, and Kamara –was also puzzling. After 20 years, they could have admitted working on the Ocean Pearl project. I also couldn't understand what had actually happened in Summerland. Ostensibly, the work of Francis's team should have strengthened oversight of the casino, but it did the opposite. So I felt that there must be other actors involved, or that the advice given was not consistent with what it was purported to be. When Sean Carroll, my partner in the detective agency, identified Chen as someone he had seen in Balabo, I knew he had to be implicated. Like Francis, he told a story that just didn't add up."

"Tim must be relieved to have the case closed. But I don't think it will save APTI. The negative publicity has forced the member governments to justify APTI's existence and to make the case for continuing to fund it, which they are reluctant to do. I'll bet that they'll use this occasion to pull the plug on the organization."

"As I said at the party for Francis, in my view it's served its purpose, but the world has moved on."

"I think you're right." She frowned. "Changing the subject, poor Adele has lost both her friend Bob and husband Francis. I went to see her the other day, to console her, but she seems inconsolable for the moment. I expect she'll get over it, though. She'll soon have men flocking around her, and that will cheer her up. I don't think she really loved Francis. She was enchanted at first by a life where she could have all the material things she coveted. But I think after a while she found it boring, which is why she started seeing Bob."

"At least Giroux no longer treats her as a suspect. He is proud as a peacock now, having solved the case with my help, which he acknowledges. I don't begrudge him his glory."

"Well, Hamish, I expect we won't be seeing each other anymore. But should you come again to Ottawa, I hope you'll look me up." She gave him a peck on the cheek.

ASHCROFT-BY-THE-SEA, DEC. 25

Hamish and Sean were hosting friends Izzie French and Marjoree Price for Christmas dinner at The Oaks. The front door of the house was decorated with garlands of holly leaves, and electric candles shone on the sills of the windows. The dining room had a fir tree in a corner, with the top of the tree touching the eight-foot-high ceiling. It was covered by festive decorations–silver balls and miniature boxes wrapped in green and red.

Hamish had agreed for once to cook a turkey. The large bird was well browned and filled with stuffing. A gravy boat contained the result of deglazing the roasting pan with port wine and thickening the sauce with flour. Wild rice and cranberry sauce were already on the table.

"How nice to get together once again," Marjoree said. "The two of you have certainly been busy since the summer! I've hardly seen you, Sean, in the last four months. How did you like your exotic travels?"

"It was good to get home. I could see spending more time in Nassau, but not in Balabo or Macau. In fact, I was very glad to leave both of them!"

Izzie gave Hamish a friendly poke in the arm. "You were going to work on that fraud case, but you got completely sidetracked, so I had to pitch in. But at least you did manage to assist the police in capturing the criminals in Ottawa, after Sean provided the key to the puzzle. Obviously, the name Summerland gives a false idea of what the country is really like these days!"

"Yes, the police found some incriminating evidence in Clarence Chen's apartment that he had taken from Bob's cottage. After killing him, he went to Bob's bedroom and removed some papers, including a copy of the report that the team had prepared and presented informally to the Summerlanders. I think that Bob knew more about the Ocean Pearl project than he revealed to us at the party. He must have realized that a comparison of this report with the advice actually given to the Summerlanders implicated the team that had worked on the project, and he didn't want to divulge yet that he had a copy. But Clarence may have guessed that he had it. I wondered why neither that report nor the one that Francis himself drafted was in Bob's files. Inspecteur Giroux tells me that Clarence has now confessed to Bob's murder. He'll likely get sentenced to life imprisonment."

"What about Armbrister? Is he happy with the outcome? And did his daughter Amelia get what she needed for her thesis?" Izzie had been following the case thanks to the occasional conversation with Hamish about it.

Sean answered for him. "Yes, Kevin Armbrister is very grateful to us for having located Amelia and brought her out safely from Summerland. He topped up the invoice we billed him with another thousand dollars. He's also grateful that the case has improved his chances of getting back his mine there. He's now making a pitch to the Summerlanders for his company to restart operations in the country, in particular to exploit the lithium deposits on the land where he once had the mining concession. Now that Summerland is opening up to the outside world, they can't avoid the issue of compensating him for expropriating it. The Summerlanders are increasingly wary of the Chinese, and the revelations concerning Sir Harold Feenstra's machinations have not helped the reputation of Xanadu Mining. The monopoly given to it by the Summerland government has been revoked, and the Mining Commission is now considering other options. Reinstating Truro Resources' mining permits looks like the best alternative all-round, since it would lead Armbrister to drop his claim for compensation. As for Amelia, she's decided once she's finished her thesis to write a history of APTI."

Hamish added: "Tim Blacket was enthusiastic when I suggested it to him, and the Institute will make her a generous advance. She has some insights into the history of Summerland that few others have, and she knows how to write it up in a way that makes it accessible to a lay person. This could well be the start of a stellar academic career for her."

Izzie pursued the subject: "And what did you get from all of this, Hamish, aside from the opportunity to connect with former colleagues?"

Hamish paused to think, and said with a smile, "I was struck by how even people with a reputation for probity succumb to the temptation to bend the laws in order to get what they want.

Many proclaim a profound devotion to virtue, but in private revel in vice."

Looking slyly at Sean, he added: "Often lust is to blame. You just have to pick up the newspaper to learn that another politician, actor, or chief executive has stupidly risked his career through sexual shenanigans. Francis Chastain seems to have been driven by lust to get the money he needed to convince Adele to marry him. He'll be forever remembered not for his achievements but for his shady dealings in Summerland."

He laughed: "As for myself, I was guided solely by the desire to see justice done and was not swayed one bit by the offer of generous compensation to take on the case!"

Sean couldn't resist saying, "At least now I'll have some money to repair the plumbing in this old house!"

About the Author

I am a retired economist living in Niagara-on-the-Lake, Ontario, and have published many books and articles in various branches of economics, including with respect to Africa.

My hobbies include gardening, kayaking, hiking, and sailing.

For more information about my detective series, *The ABC Files,* please visit **paulmassonwebsite.com**. I would welcome your feedback: you can email me using the "Contact Us" form there. To receive advance notice of new novels and a prequel of the *ABC Files* click the Newsletter sign up button.

My detective novels can be found on Amazon and on Goodreads, as well as in selected bookstores. If you enjoyed the book, please consider submitting a review on the above sites.